WINGS OF EARTH

SCATTER

THE

WINDS

OTHER WORKS

WINGS OF EARTH

SCATTER

THE

WINDS

ERIC MICHAEL CRAIG

Cover Design: Ducky Smith

PUBLISHED BY

Rivenstone Press

ISBN: 978-1-7346760-2-0

CHAPTER ONE

"ALL HANDS REPORT TO STATIONS. Code Red. This is not a drill. ExO and Payload Steward report to Operations. All hands report to stations. Code Red." Captain Valleri's voice echoed across the mess hall.

"What's a Code Red?" Kylla Torrance asked, jumping up to follow the ExO out past stunned crew and passengers, who scrambled down the hallway as if the end of the universe was gnawing at their heels.

Code Red? That can't be good.

The ExO hurled herself down the corridor. "Raiders," she hissed over her shoulder.

Tall, and built like an overly engineered wall of muscle, Ayanna Santore moved with surprising agility, rebounding off a bulkhead as she took the stairs, three at a time to reach the OpsDeck five flights above the Commons. By the time the two women leapt out onto the deck, Ayanna was a dozen strides ahead of Kylla.

The floor plating lurched upward as the primary drive cut out and they were back in normal space. Even with her limited experience in interstellar travel, Kylla recognized the feel of the field collapsing.

That obviously wasn't a normal drop into sublight.

Both women stumbled forward as emergency bulkheads clanged shut somewhere behind them.

"We're on backup power," the ExO growled, catching herself on the edge of the hatch to the Operations Deck and waiting for the Cargo Steward to catch up. She held the door open with her back while the pneumatics fought her to a stalemate. Waving Kylla through, she jumped onto the OpsDeck at the same time. The hatch slammed shut behind her.

Captain Valleri stood motionless on the command riser staring at the main viewscreen. "Is only one ship, and no match for *Agamemnon*. Da?"

"What do they want?" Kylla asked.

"Is obvious," he said. "They are pirate. We have cargo." He turned and stared at the optic protruding through her cheek orifice. "Is why I wanted you here."

She knew the extra hole in her face distracted people, and she usually tried to keep it from being annoying. Usually. But she gave it a little flick with the edge of her tongue, and it twitched as she winked at him. "Have they made any demands?"

"Only that we stop. Demand was made with pulse mine." He swung back to face the screen and shook his head.

"Are they alone?" Santore asked. She'd taken up a position behind the helmsman and was looking over his shoulder.

"We've got no one else for at least a light-year," the sensor officer answered from the far side of the deck.

"Seems arrogant for something the size of a science vessel to jump a ship this big, doesn't it?" Kylla asked. The *Agamemnon* had a crew of 250 and was carrying almost a thousand passengers. "They're thin on manpower to run a raid. You've got them two to one, even without my people."

"Da, but little science vessel has big pirate gun hidden in

hold. And bigger reactor to feed it," the captain said. He tapped the surface of his control pad and an EM scan overlaid the image on the main screen. It showed a lot of power going to a weapon mount in the belly of the ship.

"Captain, we're being hailed," the comm officer announced.

"*Viper*, to Colonial Freighter *Agamemnon*. Stand down and prepare to be boarded."

"He can't be serious," the ExO said. "He has to know we've got enough firepower to hold him off all day."

"It will depend on what is hiding in belly of little whale. Engineering, how long until main reactor is restored?" the captain asked.

"Thirty seconds."

"Until then, is moot," Valleri said. "No power, means no guns."

"And he's putting a megawatt into that weapon, whatever it is," the sensor officer said. She had to be pushing her words through a wall of acid, but in spite of that her voice sounded calm. "That could do a lot of damage, even if he doesn't hit a critical system."

"*Agamemnon*, you have ten seconds to surrender or we will open fire."

"Open audio," the captain said. "Captain Grigor Valleri of *Agamemnon* to pirate vessel. Answer is no. We will not surrender." He slashed a finger across his throat to mute the comm.

The doors opened on the *Viper*'s weapons bay and the gun swung up into sight.

"Frak. That's a particle cannon. If he's pushing a megawatt into it, he's going to feed us to the vacuum," Santore said.

"I assume that changes the playing field a little?" Kylla asked, nervously flicking the edge of her optic with her tongue. She stopped when the captain glared at it. It was a bad idea to be distracting him.

Valleri crossed his arms over his chest and tapped his foot several times before he let out a slow hissing breath. Without main power, they couldn't do much other than sit and wait to die. And staring down the emitter of a particle cannon made death a lot more relevant consideration.

"What is range?" he asked.

"Two thousand klick," the helmsman said. "Out of reach for us, but easily in his."

"Fifteen seconds," the engineer announced.

"We need to take advantage away from him," he said, nodding as he leapt over to the helm control and leaned forward to punch in a string of commands.

"Understood?" he asked as his helmsman watched curiously.

"Aye, Captain," he said, grinning.

"Open audio to *Viper*," he ordered, turning toward the comm officer.

"Channel open."

"Is Captain Valleri. State your terms for surrender."

"Valleri, there are no terms. Surrender is unconditional."

"We are carrying passengers—"

"Do you not understand the word *unconditional*?" the pirate asked.

"I do," he said. "I am offering passengers in exchange for—"

"What?" Kylla gasped, fighting down a sudden scalding rage. *He wouldn't dare.*

He snapped a finger up to silence her outburst. "Da, we carry important passengers who would swing big chit."

"We will have your passengers anyway," the captain of the *Viper* said.

"They are worth more alive, no?"

"You're threatening to vent them? You haven't got the eggs."

"If you attack, particle cannon will vent much. Our emergency systems are not in such good repair. It would be shame if no one survives. Da?"

The lights on the Operations Deck flickered as main power came back up, and she realized what was going on.

Valleri had been stalling.

He slashed across his throat again and grabbed the back of the helmsman's chair. "Now, Mr. Klinestrom!"

The officer slapped his hand down on the console and the *Aggie* lunged toward the *Viper*. At least as much as a thousand-meter-long barge could lunge at anything. It certainly wasn't fast.

But it was unexpected. And probably more than a little intimidating.

Obviously, that was what the captain had counted on.

The *Viper* twisted away to avoid the charging bulk, opening it up to a strafing run across the top of its hull with the belly lasers of the *Agamemnon*.

The repelling guns of the colonial freighter weren't powerful, but at close range they were enough. And there were dozens of them.

Most of the beams did minimal damage, but the sheer number meant that there were bound to be some critical hits.

A power coupling on the particle cannon's mounting cradle was one of the first casualties. Spinning wildly, the crippled support hardware bought them several precious seconds as they drove forward across the enemy ship.

Another laser split a cooling line to the primary reactor, spewing a spectacular cloud of vapor over their targeting sensors and the cannon's aperture. Unfortunately for the crew of the *Viper*, that happened in the same instant that its weapons officer fired. The heat of the dense fog turning to plasma, fused the end of the cannon and sent a feedback surge through their systems.

It was pure luck. But it worked, and the *Agamemnon* accelerated to cruise and away before the pirate raider's power grid overloaded and slagged their primary transfer manifold.

"Are they pursuing?" Santore barked as she spun to face the sensor station.

"Negative, it looks like they took heavy collateral damage," she said. "They're dead in space."

"Once they make repairs, they'll be in pursuit."

"Da," the captain said. "Set course for Kentaurus Colony."

"We aren't going to Kentaurus," Kylla said quietly, shaking her head. It was a fact that only she and the captain shared for the moment.

"No, we are not," he confirmed, turning to face her, and matching her tone. "But they do not know that, and we must appear to be running for safety."

His expression reminded her of her first husband Edison when he was trying to teach her something that she thought she already knew. She shook off his memory and cocked her head to the side, flicking at her optic and watching as his gaze locked onto it.

He nodded, closing his eyes, and letting out a breath before he explained himself. "We cannot outrun pirate vessel, but while they make repairs, we can possibly get sufficient distance to exceed their sensors. Then we will correct course and be about our business. Is good plan, no?"

Not really, she thought to herself as she stared at the distorted ring of stars through the viewscreen.

But it's probably our only option.

CHAPTER TWO

"Valleri is not bad, as captains go," Kylla said as she came through the door.

"He shouldn't be, he's an old man," Dorran said, glancing up at her as she tossed her thinpad on the table. They shared one of the few semi-private quarters in Passenger Ward One. Privacy didn't matter much, since the Ward was just a huge cargo hold with modular walls and mesh decks. Fortunately, it had ventilation for the most part. It wasn't enough to keep the pheromone fog down, but at least the air was breathable, despite the intense human funk.

"Mr. James, I should put you over my knee," she said, rolling her best hairy eyeball in his direction. "I'm old enough to have grandkids Valleri's age."

He scanned her physique as she shimmied her over-vest off her shoulders. "I'm not usually into that, but I could be convinced in your case," he said, winking.

She might have been that old, but she also knew there was no way to tell by looking at her. She almost shivered as the cool air washed over her thinskin undersuit.

He tried to fight back a smile but failed. "Best genes on the market, chit for chit," he said, nodding appreciatively.

She turned to the VAT and filled a bottle of gojuice for herself. "You forget, I'm not like you. I was born and then rebuilt. You came out of the box engineered."

"Even so, you don't look a day over 110 standard."

She tapped the mounting loose from her bicuspid and rolled the optic implant out of her mouth. She stuck her tongue out through the hole in her cheek and wagged it at him. "You are such a brat."

"Did I say something wrong?" He grinned in a mockery of innocence. "You know you still make the mundanes crazy."

Fortunately, that much was still true. At 141, she could pass for thirty-ish. She turned more eyeballs than average, despite her actual age. But she always thought her appeal was the result of experience. Lots of it.

Walking across the small room, she set her bottle down on the shelf beside her bed. Peeling off her waist wrap, she tossed it on the chair and crashed down on the end of her bunk. "So that Code Red was almost a bad thing," she said, leaning forward and resting her elbows on her knees.

"I scanned that much," he said, suddenly getting serious to match her change in tone. "Someone said it was pirates?"

She nodded. "It felt like amateurs to me. They overreached a long way trying to jump a colonial freighter, but they might have just been a poke to see what we tasted like."

"You think they'll be back?"

"I'd count on it," she said with a snort. "Valleri stuffed their ego in a bag this time, but that probably made for a general foul mood on their ship."

"I understand pirates tend to be the grudgy sort," he said.

"I know I was," she said, pulling her lips sidewise into a grin.

He obviously didn't know if he should take her at her word. At her age, anything was possible. Even a stint at piracy.

Instead of asking, he tipped an eyebrow to its inquisitive setting and waited for her to explain. Or not.

She chose not.

"What happened?" he asked, after almost a minute of hanging silence.

"A small raider dropped a pulse mine in our path and we ran over it. It knocked us out of cruise long enough for this puny-ass, former science vessel, to waggle his little penis in our face. He was carrying a big enough gun to be respectable but didn't have the eggs to go with it."

He nodded. "A pulse mine. That explains the power bounce in the Creche Sequencer and Incubators."

"That's where I wanted to lean with this conversation," she admitted. "Did it do any damage to the systems?"

"Not to the Creche or the reactor, but it knocked Solo into the hole," he said. "I was running a diagnostic on the code controller interface when he burped."

Dorran was their lead engineer, so it was fortunate he was on duty when it happened. If anything had gone wrong, they could have lost the whole Creche run. "Did you get everything back online?"

"It didn't even all go down before the resets kicked, so I'd wager none of the neural-classes even noticed. They were in a cool-down session when it happened."

"What about Solo?"

He lowered his voice and nodded. "It only took a peripheral reload since the quantum core didn't reboot. It might have been a few milliseconds for the awareness processor to reestablish comm. This distributed awareness code is a lot more resilient than the older AA core codes."

"It's also still illegal," she said, glaring at him for even bringing it up. Because the Odysseus Awareness nearly destroyed humanity trying to save it, the Coalition had made the creation of distributed artificial awareness a capital crime. It was one of the few offenses the Charter set out as automatically punishable by execution.

He shrugged her reaction off. But since she'd been on the bleeding edge of things when the Odysseus War started, it wasn't something she took lightly.

That experience was why Welcor put her in charge of the Novus Division of the Augment Program.

"What about our reactor? The *Aggie's* went down."

"When it hit, we were working through the systems diagnostic. We had the secondary antimatter injectors online and ready to test, but even if we hadn't, the antimatter containment on our reactor would only have needed to re-init," he said. "As it worked out, I think the end-to-end blink was under ten seconds."

"It took the ship's engineers over a minute to restart," she said.

"That's frakking miraculous for a barge like this," he said, his face showing his surprise. "If it took them under an hour to get the coils recharged, I'd be impressed. The *Agamemnon* has a huge power grid, and it's all antique hardware."

She was well into her sixth decade before the Coalition launched the first interstellar colonial transports. She stared at him for several seconds before he realized he'd stepped into the recycler again.

At least, he had the grace to look embarrassed when he caught her glare.

"Is there any way we can protect against this kind of problem if it happens again?" she asked, winking, and letting him off the hook.

"I don't know, but our gear is all top tier. A cold start-up from scratch would only take a few minutes. The Incubators might go into shut down before then, but we still wouldn't be looking at damage to the system, or the Creche run. At least as far as I know."

"If we have to pull the run, we'd have to renormalize their maturation rate," she said. "I know back in the dark ages, they used to do that step manually, but now it's all part of the main-sequence programming."

"Even at a twenty to one maturation rate, I think they'd do fine for a short stretch, but you might want to talk it over with the medical team. I'm not an expert on how long they can be out of the tube before it's a situation to worry over."

She glared at the deck plating under her feet.

"And… you think this might be a problem we'll face?" he asked, leaning forward, and trying to make eye contact.

She didn't look up but let out a long hissing breath before she nodded. "Once we were moving again, and out of immediate danger, I talked it over with Ayanna Santore. She wasted no air in saying we were lucky it was only a single mine this time. It was an amateur mistake on their part."

"The ExO would know, but I don't scan," he said, shaking his head.

"Pirates usually spread pulse mines in what she called a field-array. If we'd gotten into one of those we wouldn't have gotten out."

"Did she explain how that swings?"

"An arrayed mine field delays the first pulse until the target is deep inside it," she said. "Once they snag a ship, then the mines go into a regular cycle of discharging EM pulses. Every minute or so another wave goes off. Apparently, a network of mines working together can keep a ship from being able to restore primary power indefinitely."

"Yah, that would do it," he said, grinding at an eye with his knuckle.

"Is there any way we can protect our systems against it?"

"Not run into it?" He pushed himself back in his chair and sucked a lip between his teeth to chew on it. "There are too many variables to constrain to give you an effective answer."

"What variables?" she asked. "Maybe I can get some data for you to work with."

"How many mines? The discharge interval? The amplitude? The frequency? The spacing of the field?"

"Without that, we're whiffing?"

He shrugged. "We can leave the secondaries in test mode and shorten our reset time, but even with that, I'd wager hard that if we get caught in a web of linked mines, we're hammered right along with the *Aggie*."

CHAPTER THREE

IT HAD BEEN a long shift, on the butt-side of another long shift. With no sleep the night before either. Ayanna Santore had just hit the corridor to the officer's quarters when her commlink chirped. *Frak.*

"ExO," she said, stopping to lean her forehead against a structural bulkhead.

"Commander, report to my quarters," the captain said. His voice sounded almost as tired as she felt.

"Yes, Sir," she said, tapping out of the comm and thumping her head against the steel beam several times. "He probably wants me to feed his fricking monkey," she muttered as she pushed herself away

"Is that what they call it now?" Jason Willis teased as he passed her on the way to his quarters. The Chief Engineer had been on duty at least as long as she had, and the set of his shoulders said he was aiming for a long hot shower and nothing was going to get in his way.

Except the chirp of his own commlink.

He coasted to a stop and dropped his head with a heavy sigh as he smacked his link. "I'm in bed," he lied.

"Is not true," Valleri said. "Report to my quarters immediately."

"Aye, Captain," he said, spinning to follow her.

Dropping into step with her, he sighed again. "'In his quarters' means it's not urgent. Why can't it wait until firstshift?"

"Because he's the boss," she said. "And he probably likes the idea of both of us double-teaming his monkey." She rolled an eye in his direction as he groaned at the thought.

It didn't help that when they got to the door to the captain's quarters, Kroshka opened it. Valleri was a peculiar man, even without his bizarre taste in animal companions. The brown spider monkey had been his pet for most of his adult life, and he often let it do things for him. Like answer the door and serve drinks.

Being a cloned reproduction of a once extinct animal was strange enough, but this creature liked no one, and often barked and screamed when it encountered any human other than the captain. This time was no exception, as the ear-piercing screech threatened to send both officers running back down the hall.

"Kroshka! Quiet!" the captain bellowed, pointing to her sleep cage and glaring.

The foul tempered primate spun and waved its backside and hairy tail at them obscenely before it darted off to sulk. To both their dismay, the sound it made before departing left no doubt that it had also deployed an ugly cloud like a gaseous force field.

Obviously, it had been saving whatever it was for days.

Jason gasped, blinking several times in shock, and wiping tears from his face with the back of his hand. "Shit, that's worse than a blown recycler line."

"There's a reason I call that bitch *Kakashka*," Santore whispered, holding her breath, and pushing past the evil stench.

"Kash… what?" he asked, choking as he braved the toxic wall and followed her into the room.

The captain laughed. "Da is good name. I did not know you

spoke Russkiy."

"I don't, but I figured it would be polite to be able to swear at your girlfriend in a language she understands," she said with a shrug.

"What's it mean?" the engineer asked.

"Turd," the captain supplied with an approving nod.

"In polite company," she added.

Valleri gestured toward the sitting area and grabbed a bottle and glasses from his liquor cabinet before he walked over to join them.

She shook her head. At least he wasn't making the hairy turd-slinger bring the drinks.

"Vodka? I'm not going to like this, am I?" she asked, sitting down, and watching while he poured three tall shots. She'd served with the captain long enough to know that when he brought out the bottle before he started talking, it wasn't a good sign.

"Is good Vodka," he said, managing to look offended that she wouldn't like his preferred alcohol.

"That's not what I meant, and you know it," she said. "Anesthetic for what you called us here to discuss?"

He rocked his head back and forth several times before he reached down and picked up his glass. He waited for them to follow his lead.

"Na zdorov'ye," he said, pitching back his glass.

"Yah, to your health too." She took a respectable swallow, but Jason just wet his lips. He wasn't much of a social drinker.

"Now, what's swinging that you need to numb the pain?" she asked once her voice returned. Vodka wasn't her favorite intoxicant, especially at this combustibility level.

"Da, is true. You will not approve, I think." he said, leaning forward and setting his glass on the table between them. He didn't refill it, but he pushed the bottle in her direction. "We are off original flight plan."

"What do you mean we are off the flight plan?"

"Exactly as I said. We are diverting to 127 G Centauri."

Jason slipped a thinpad out of his pocket and called up the navigation chart data to scan the file on their new destination. "That's almost twenty light-years out of our way," he said, handing it to the ExO after he'd skimmed the info.

"Eighteen," Valleri corrected.

"It's past Kentaurus no matter how you shove it," she said, putting the thinpad down beside her glass and topping up its contents. "This says it's an unsurveyed binary system."

"Is listed as unsuitable for colonization," he said. "Is different, no?"

"We're not a survey ship," Jason said.

She glanced at the engineer and nodded. "Jace is right. What the hell are we doing?"

"Following orders. We are to deliver passengers to seventh planet and provide unloading support for hardware."

She let out a blast of air and picked up her glass. It didn't help as she slammed it back. "Why?"

"Is not my place to question."

"I thought they were going to one of the moons of Kentaurus," she said. "It was supposed to be a drop and run. We're light on cargo handlers for a deployment."

He waved his hand dismissively. "Is small outpost. Science equipment and habitat only."

"A thousand people and two cargo bays of gear is not a small outpost," Jason said. In truth, as colony start-ups went, it was on the light side, but it didn't change the fact that they were thin-staffed for that kind of operation.

"Will only require layover of one week."

"Not unless they have their own dropship pilots," he said.

She nodded. "He's right, we're way skinny on those, too."

"Da, they do," he said. "They will drive our loaders."

"Who authorized that?"

The captain refilled his glass. "Is in mission charter."

"Somebody's melted a chip," she said, shaking her head.

"I have to agree with her," the engineer added. "We sure don't need club fingered grounders smashing our hardware. I can barely keep it all running as it stands."

He shrugged, handing her the bottle, and letting her load another shot.

"Why wasn't this in the flight plan?" she asked. "Frak, why wasn't this in the officer's briefing?"

"I do not know. Charter ordered captain-level confidentiality on mission until time to deviate from course."

"This stinks like your monkey's ass," she growled. Alcohol-fueled anger boiled up through her.

He shook his head. "Is unusual, but not without precedent."

"Screw that. We work for the government. We're not supposed to do shady shit."

The captain raised an eyebrow. That was all it took.

"Fine," she said, almost laughing at the idiocy of her own statement. "Governments are the source of shady shit."

"But that doesn't make her wrong," Jason agreed. "This is way out of spec."

"At the very least we should file an amended flight plan with FleetCom and cover our eggs," she said.

"No flight plan updates are authorized," Valleri said. "Is in orders as well."

"Nojo?" She blinked several times before she could throttle back enough to continue talking in complete sentences. "We've already crossed up with a raider, and if FleetCom doesn't know where we are, we're frakking humped dry if they come after us again."

"If pirates come after us, we are humped as it is, no?" he said.

Unfortunately, that was the truth. The Coalition had expanded out in long, thin streamers of civilization. Like the ancient highways of Earth, civilization popped up along the transportation corridors, but there was a lot of open emptiness between destinations. And it took a long time to get anywhere. Even in a shiny-ass FleetCom Multicruiser.

"Centauri Sector is frontier. FleetCom cannot police every parsec. Their job is just to collect bodies pirates leave behind."

"What this distills down to is whether we're carrying anything valuable enough to fight over," Santore said.

"For pirates, even food is valuable enough to kill for," Jason said quietly.

"Yah, but is anything in our cargo worth dying for?"

The captain shrugged. "I do not know. However, not knowing is standard procedure when employed by government."

"If it was my choice, I'd be out of here in a microbeat," she said, realizing that it was true. If they weren't so far into the black, she'd turn in her commission. She was tired of Valleri and his fucking monkey.

"Da. Is not your choice. And is not our decision."

She downed the shot of vodka and glared at him for several seconds before she turned her attention to Kroshka. The monkey was sitting in the door to her sleep cage, probably plotting her next turd-hurling escapade. She hated that animal, and even though it wasn't the source of her immediate frustration, she glared.

Without a doubt, Kroshka understood what she was thinking, and scurried off into its bed to hide.

Finally, she turned back to Valleri. Clearing her throat, she asked, "When do we cross over to the realm of stupid?"

"Is not as bad as it sounds," the captain said. "Helm set new heading once we had exceeded sensor range of *Viper*."

"I wonder how much chit it took to swing this deal. It's our bag in the wind out here, and I just hope to frak that someone remembers our next of kin when the debt collects." Glancing at Jason, she could tell he agreed with her even if he wouldn't say it so bluntly.

"Thank you for the vodka, but if that's all, Captain?"

He looked at the bottle. It was still half full. "Is more, if it would help?" he offered.

She shook her head and stood up stiffly. "No, Sir. If you don't mind, I'd like to get some horizontal time before I'm due on deck."

He nodded and waved toward the door. "Da."

There isn't enough vodka on the ship to make me feel better about this situation, she thought as she glanced at Kroshka to make sure it was safe to make her exit. The beast was still hiding under her covers.

I guess she's smarter than she looks.

CHAPTER FOUR

Firstmeal was an odd ritual on the *Agamemnon*, but this morning it felt exceptionally strange. Word had spread through the passengers that they'd had a run in with a pirate raider, and everyone was off balance.

The passengers under Kylla's command ate in a separate dining hall, and only she had permission to eat in the crew section of the ship. Officially, as Payload Steward, while they were in space, she held a position on the ship's roster and the rest of her people were legally just cargo. Coalition law considered colonists another commodity, no different from hardware in a legal perspective.

To keep some semblance of harmony, Kylla took most of her meals in the Ward cafeteria, and only had secondmeal in the officer's mess. She sliced a delicate line between maintaining her responsibility to the crew and the morale of her people. Today things were tense, and she expected to be dealing with a lot of uncertainty.

Ayanna Santore showing up and aiming for her specifically, was not one of the things she'd anticipated. The ExO usually sat the first watch in Ops. For her to be anywhere else on the ship this early in the morning was a sign of a bigger problem than pirates.

Like perhaps they had fallen into a black hole.

"May I join you?" she asked, walking up and setting a cup of pseudojo on the table. It smelled like acid and looked like it was trying to smoke its way out of the cup. The ExO held a second cup in her hand, so obviously she intended it to be a gesture of kindness. Kylla always enjoyed a good cup of coffee, but this wasn't even close.

"Of course," she said, sliding the cup back far enough that she wasn't in danger of the vapors destroying her sense of smell. "What brings you down to the slums?"

Santore glanced at the others sitting at the table and raised an eyebrow before she sat down. Clearly what she had to say wasn't for general consumption. "In private? Please."

Kylla bristled at the implication that her people weren't trustworthy, but she nodded. Everyone got up but Dorran. He'd just landed with his tray. Tapping his arm to make sure he looked at her, she twitched her optic with her tongue and winked.

I'll record the conversation, she didn't say, but he understood.

"I don't think this is food anyway," he said, pushing his meal back and standing.

"Make sure Solo is online. I've got work to do in the Sequencer Lab as soon as we're done here," she said. She knew that there was nothing she was qualified to do with the hardware, but he picked up on what she meant.

Have Solo link to my optic. I want it listening.

He nodded, disappearing into the crowd. The ExO watched after him until she was sure he was far enough away not to hear what she had to say. Scanning the other tables to satisfy herself that nobody else was listening, she leaned forward and put her elbows on the table, propping her jaw on her fists. "You want to explain to me exactly what you're doing."

Kylla glanced around and then down at her plate. "Eating

firstmeal?" Her optic buzzed twice against her bicuspid, letting her know Solo was recording the conversation in case there was a problem later. That meant that her staff would be listening to the feed as well.

"Don't play ignorant," Santore said, dropping her expression into a stone-dead glare. "Captain Valleri just unspooled a new set of orders. I'd wager you've known all along what we were doing."

It was pointless to lie. There was no sidewise step that would make sense, nor would it be smart to try. The ExO had a lot of power on the ship and turning her into anything other than an ally would be foolish.

"Ah. We've just changed course then?" Kylla asked, nodding.

Santore's eyes narrowed and a rapid array of micro-expressions fluttered across her face before she locked the glare into place once more. "What's the real mission?"

"We're setting up a science outpost," she said. After over a hundred years of studying people, Kylla had learned to read the subtle twitches and unarticulated changes in facial expression well enough to know that a person always broadcast their thoughts. "But you've been told that already."

She nodded. "What kind of science outpost needs to be set up in secret?"

"Most of them actually," she said, leaning back in her chair and broadening her perspective to include the ExO's body language. "There's a lot of research that goes on that the general public doesn't know about. We're just one of those nameless projects."

"I get that. But what's so secret that the captain was told not to even share the mission with his officers? That's stupidly dangerous, especially when we've already had one pirate stick his nose up our ass," she said, holding her voice dead calm.

In spite of her effort to conceal her thoughts, she was sending

22

mixed signals. The dichotomy between her tone of voice and what she showed in her face, screamed that there was something else driving her.

It feels like something is… tearing?

"Aren't pirates part of life in the black?" Kylla asked, sidestepping the question. "It was one ship working alone, and he wasn't much of a threat."

Santore's eyes narrowed and her pupils dilated. "Pirates never run alone in this sector." She hauled in a breath and then shook her head. "You didn't answer the question. What are you doing? What kind of outpost is it?"

"Biomedical research," she offered, studying the ExO's face closely. Her lower eyelids shifted as she tried to hide a flash of frustration.

She's not going to give it up.

"It's the kind of project that's best done away from civilization," she added.

"Biological weapons?"

"Frak no," she said, rolling her eyes. "Ayanna, I promise you, we're not setting up a weapons lab. Is that what you're worried about?"

"Then what is it?" she pressed, letting the casual use of her first name slide by with no deflection.

"I'd rather not say," Kylla admitted.

The ExO's jaw muscles clenched slightly. *Another bad indicator.*

"My position makes me responsible for crew safety," she said, visibly trying to keep her response in check. "I'd prefer not to assert my authority, but since you've got part of cargo bay-2 locked down under a biohazard protocol, I can force you to allow an inspection of your containment procedures. For the sake of the ship."

She leaned back and spread her hands on the table in front of her, taking several slow steady breaths before she added, "Or you can just give it to me straight and quit trying to evade my question."

"Alright," Kylla said. "Welcor is working on developing an improved omnithraxin compound. What we're setting up is a genetic engineering lab to handle the genomic resequencing of a specific biological material." It was a lie, but it wasn't likely that a freighter ExO would know enough about the hard science to drag her into the dirt.

"Why does this have to be done at a secret location?" Her eyes narrowed again. She wasn't buying the explanation.

"The problem is that the process is environmentally dependent, and we need to keep the location where the work is done confidential. Corporate espionage is a big problem in pharmaceutical science," she said.

That much is true, so maybe she'll accept it at face value.

Santore shook her head.

Or not.

Lowering her voice, Kylla looked around and shrugged. "We're in final testing of a new drug, and the Science Wing of the Coalition wants us to do it on a marginally habitable planet to make sure it never gets out of containment." It was less true, but it was a fallback argument. Invoking any of the upper level Wings of Government tended to push people into submission.

Her expression showed that it had slowed her down. A little. "This is that kind of dangerous?" she asked. "Does the captain know what you're doing?" Strangely, her affect seemed to calm at the idea of it being hazardous.

"I don't know what they included in the mission charter, since I stay in the sciences and not the legal side of things," she said. "But all I can say for sure is it's not any risk, as long as we're transporting unmodified subjects."

"Subjects?"

"Yes. We have several human carriers in metabolic stasis," she said. "They're biological transport containers until we get the lab set up."

"I'm not sure I follow," the ExO said. "But it doesn't sound ethical, or legal, to use humans for experimentation like that."

"They're all volunteers, and there's no risk to them," Kylla said. "They are all carriers of an inhibited version of the Burroughs V2-A pathogen. It's non-contagious in its current state, but we need to have genetic donors to develop the Viroxycin Immunoxate variant. We're working on a cure for Sokat Reinforcement Syndrome. Until we get them into the lab we'll be setting up, and unpack their genome sequences, we can't calibrate—"

"Wait. Nevermind. Don't waste a good explanation," Santore said, holding up her hands in surrender. "You're way over my air supply."

She shrugged. "Sorry, genomic medicine is one of my passions and when you get me talking…" That was another lie. Fortunately, her doublespeak was good enough to overwhelm the ExO's desire to push on.

"I guess that explains the secrecy," she said. "What I need to know from you, is why a pirate raider would be interested in your cargo."

The tension reappeared in her face, but there was something more to it.

"I can't tell you that," Kylla said. "Other than, maybe they just don't know what the *Agamemnon* is carrying."

"That's possible, but shit don't stink like it's supposed to," she said, pushing herself up from the table. "One pirate ship tells me they were just tasting the waters. And that's sidewise."

"I'll trust your judgment on that," she said, shrugging and

standing up also. "Ayanna, I hope our conversation stays just between us. I told you more than I should have, and it could cost me my job if they find out I broke confidentiality."

Looking down at the deck, she nodded. "It's need-to-know as far as I am concerned."

"Thanks," she said as the ExO pivoted and walked away. Kylla stared after her until she left the cafeteria.

She's right, shit doesn't stink square.

She doesn't think the pirates will try again... she knows they will.

CHAPTER FIVE

KYLLA PUSHED THROUGH the inner seal on the Sequencer Control Lab. It was as close as they had to a private office aboard the *Agamemnon*. Only her staff and the med-techs who watched over the Incubators, and their occupants, got inside and past the biohazard doors. Not that there was any danger, but they had to keep up pretenses until they deployed on 127 G Centauri. It was also the only thing that kept Santore from walking in and discovering the truth of what they were doing. "We definitely have trouble chasing us," she said. "Other than the ExO."

"That is an assumption," Solo said. The immensely powerful AA was a stickler for precision. Although its progenitor understood the concept of lying, it also had imparted on Solo the value of knowing precisely when it was essential to manipulate the truth. Apparently claiming something that wasn't known as absolute fact, was one of those times where it was not acceptable.

"Am I the only one who caught that she was hiding something?" she asked, stopping and glancing at the wall screen that showed the last image from her optic rather than its usual display of the Incubators. "You saw what I saw."

"Of all of us, you're the most experienced reader," Dorran said, offering her a mug of real coffee. One of the conditions she'd given Welcor before she took the position over the Novus Division, was that they sent an ample supply of coffee. It was a luxury they always kept fresh and on hand.

"Solo should be able to interpret her biometrics better than I can, even from my limited bandwidth optic," she said, taking a seat at the end of the sequencing design console they used as a conference table.

"I concur that it appears she was attempting to conceal something, however what that may be is not clear. In each instance where the subject of your conversation turned to the potential of pirates, there was a heightened neuro-vascular response. However, that alone does not mean the pirates are coming for us. It is possible that she was concealing fear or frustration, and that triggered her reaction."

She pulled her face into a skeptical grimace. "I didn't smell fear on her."

"Over the pseudojo in your face?" the engineer asked.

She flinched at the memory of the reeking cup but shook her head.

"There's also the pheromone saturation problem with the air recyclers," Dr. Michaels pointed out as he slid into the seat beside her. "Even our own people are walking around half-blinded by it."

She shook her head again. "Santore knows something that she doesn't want anyone else to know."

"It would be possible that it is simply a matter of ship business," Solo suggested. "Captain Valleri does not have any obligation to notify us of problems unless there is an immediate risk to our safety. This would also apply to his crewmembers and officers."

"I could always see if I can get a similar reaction from Valleri," she offered.

"That might be worth trying," the doctor said, "but is it necessary? I'd be in favor of erring on the side of prudence."

"Adam's right," Dorran said. "We know we've already scraped against the darkhats. Why don't we assume that trouble is looking to bend our stiffs and just plan accordingly?"

"I don't have one of those," Kylla reminded him with a wink and a suggestive glance at the part of his anatomy at risk. "But what are you talking about doing?"

"Let's make it as hard as possible for them to catch us," he offered.

"Unless you've come up with a new FTL theory, I doubt there's much we can do to outrun a pirate raider," the doctor said.

Dorran shrugged. "Maybe we can buy time. We've only got a few more days until we get to ground. If we can get the captain to shut off the transponder, it would make us a lot harder to find."

"Running without a transponder is a violation of FleetCom regulations," Solo pointed out. "I do not believe he will consider such a course of action."

"Even if he did, Ayanna would smash his bag before we got another light-year," Kylla said. If she didn't like the captain, that might have been an amusing image, but she shook her head. "The ExO is too bound by procedures to let it swing."

"We could shut it off ourselves," he said.

"Right. And end up chained to the floor in a dark holding cell. Fun maybe, but not an idea I want to consider without a lot of saltpeter," Adam said, laughing. The doctor did have a sense of humor… sometimes.

Saltpeter? Kylla let her head flop forward. "I doubt we could get to the transponder to disable it, anyway. The transmitter antenna has to be outside, and the controls will be in Ops."

"I can access the necessary hardware," Solo offered, managing to sound meek. Obviously, it thought they were discussing a foolish plan, but it had to offer the possibility for consideration.

"I didn't know you had access to the ship systems at that level?" Dorran asked.

"I have been utilizing deep-comm access through the synchronization channel of the navigation beacon system. I have used it to maintain a portion of my distributed awareness with the Primary AA in Zone One."

"You can do that without being detected?" she asked, concerned that the AA might have exposed them.

"Yes. Distributed Awareness requires real time comm, and although that is not possible at this range, a continuous bidirectional communication link allows for an approximation of the effect."

"That has to be a strain on your cyber psychology," the doctor said.

"It creates an unsettling plurality of awareness, but since we anticipated this, it is nothing that cannot be tolerated. Once we can determine a means of instantaneous communication, it will be a non-issue."

"That's all on tomorrow's worry list, but you're saying you already have access to the transponder and haven't been detected?" she asked.

"That is correct. The ship's AA is an older Quanticom Series-10. It is not a challenge to remain unnoticed at this level of infiltration," Solo said, pulling off a good approximation of smugness.

"What would you have to do to shut it down?" she asked.

"Currently, the ship's AA is operating near capacity controlling the field dynamics of the cruise engines. Any additional load would exceed its capacity."

"And slag the coils," Dorran added.

"The coils would not be damaged," Solo argued.

"Even though FTL field propulsion isn't in my air mix, it's basic physics that any object moving above light velocity, without a stabilized inertial charge, becomes infinitely massive. I think that makes us a black hole in most universes."

"That would be bad," Kylla said. "And it would probably qualify as frakking the coils."

"But in that case, we wouldn't care," he admitted.

"So, overloading the ship's AA is a bad idea," Adam said.

"I was suggesting that I could force the ship's core processor utilization level up incrementally through a series of diagnostic interrogations," Solo explained. "When it reaches its operational maximum, it would be possible to overload the transponder subsystems without being directly detected."

"You're saying you could distract it and then fuse a support system to take it offline? Without it seeing you coming?" the engineer asked, pulling the corner of his mouth sidewise into a mischievous grin. "Cybernetic sleight-of-hand."

"Precisely," Solo said.

"Can you display the transponder system?" he asked. An instant later, the circuit diagram appeared in the middle of the console table. "If I remember right, this should be a straight-out high-power gravity spectrum transmitter. If we can open a signal pathway across the primary feed from anywhere inside its main amplifier conduit, it would scorch anything that took the load. The current levels are all isolated..." His voice trailed off as he started tapping ideas into the diagram.

"Wouldn't they know we did it?" Kylla asked, watching the engineer planning his mayhem with amusement. It was a serious risk to contemplate sabotaging a ship in space, but he seemed to be enjoying the idea. *Maybe too much.*

"Once we decide where to strike the system, I can delete evidence of my intrusion, and leave a trail that would indicate the *Agamemnon*'s AA caused the failure," Solo suggested. "In doing so, it would force the crew to do a system-wide diagnostic of the core controllers before they could consider bringing the transponder back online. This would undoubtedly take a day or more depending on the crew's efficiency."

"What does that get us?" the doctor asked.

"It would effectively make us invisible outside of active sensor range," it said. "The *Agamemnon*'s cruise engines are relatively low power and only emit gravimetric radiation that would be detectable for a half light-year."

Dorran glanced up, but his voice sounded like he was somewhere else. "Bigger coils, like the ones on pirate ships, are visible much farther. We could see them a lot sooner than they could see us."

"That would be helpful," Kylla said.

"Unfortunately, if the *Agamemnon*'s transponder is disabled, and the crew cannot fix it on location, the appropriate procedure would be to make port at the nearest repair facility." Solo almost sounded disappointed.

"Kentaurus," she said, puckering her mouth into a frown. "How do we convince Valleri not to do that?"

"Does that mean you're signing off on this?" the engineer asked, this time without looking up.

She drew in a long, slow breath and fiddled with her optic while she mulled the idea over. "Not yet," she said. "But being harder to spot does have some advantages."

"That is probably how you convince him," Adam said, leaning back in his chair and drumming his fingers on the edge of the console table. "Get him to realize that, if the transponder stays offline for a few days, it serves everyone's interest."

"Additionally, if you can integrate the ExO's concerns regarding pirate pursuit into the calculation, you should be able to move him in the right direction."

"True that is," she said. "Ayanna might not back the idea, but that doesn't mean she can't be used against him."

CHAPTER SIX

"CAPTAIN VALLERI, please report to Operations." It was the helmsman, and his voice sounded like his eggs were in a crusher.

Tapping his collarcomm, the captain growled, "Da, Mr. Klinestrom, what is problem?"

He and Kylla were sitting in his ready room discussing their upcoming deployment plans. Because of their detour, they were still two days out from 127 G Centauri, but the fact that it was her people who would pilot the dropships, made the whole operation unusual in his mind. He wanted to make sure that things went smoothly.

Of course, it would have been normal procedure for the ExO to handle the arrangements with one of her people, but Kylla had planned to invade the captain's space when she was sure he was on duty, and not Santore. The arrangements were secondary in her mind at the moment.

Even without her extraordinary perception, it was obvious that he enjoyed her company. Her pheromones made sure of it. His eyes hadn't wandered from somewhere well below her chin in the last several minutes, and he seemed to sink deeper into the fog, the longer they sat alone in his office.

Which was also part of her plan.

She knew what Klinestrom was about to report, since Solo had vibrated her optic to signal that they were ready. She held her expression carefully curious, but not overly concerned. It would have been a serious mistake to reveal any awareness of what was coming.

"Our navigational transponder just went offline," the helmsman said. "It's hard down."

"What is wrong with it?" he asked, tearing his eyes away from her, and shaking his head as he stood up.

"It looks like the AA was doing an update to the control interface and shorted out the amplifier control circuit. It's flatlined on all diagnostics."

Heading out into the OpsDeck, he gestured for her to follow. "Is damage repairable?"

The commlink dropped and Klinestrom's voice carried across the deck as they approached. "Engineering reports they have a repair team suiting up to go outside and do a physical inspection. Until they get eyeballs on it, they won't know."

"We should stand down from cruise until they have looked it over," Valleri said, stopping in the center of the command riser. It wasn't quite an order, as he stated it, and the helmsman waited.

Fortunately.

It would have made things a lot harder for Kylla to push her agenda if they were already standing still.

She stopped a half-step behind the captain and leaned in closer, pausing for almost a full second to make sure her pheromones caught up with them. "May I suggest that it might not be a good idea to stop," she offered. "If there are pirates—"

"Respectfully, ma'am," Santore said, appearing out of nowhere, "Although you might legally be a member of this crew while you are the Cargo Steward, command decisions are not within your scope of authority." She'd apparently come into Ops from the main corridor and stood behind them, watching.

Frak! Why is she here?

"Excuse me?" Kylla said, spinning and trying to put on an air of indignation. It didn't help that she knew the ExO was right, but she glued her best condescending mask into place and pushed back with the superiority it gave her. "Weren't you the one who came to me about concerns that the *Viper* was sniffing us out? If we stand down from cruise, you might as well send out the invitations and ask them to come party."

"It isn't relevant if pirates are in the area, it's FleetCom protocol to hold position to make repairs if the ship's transponder is offline," she stated flatly.

Kylla turned back to the captain, intentionally cutting Santore out of the conversation. "If we can do the repairs without stopping, I think there's no logical reason for us to be a stationary target. Ayanna pointed out just this morning that she thinks the *Viper* might have been an exploratory probe. If that's true, there will be others out here with them and they will certainly be looking for us."

The captain stepped over and leaned against his seat. It moved him a bit farther from her zone of hormonal influence, but his face said he was tilting in her direction anyway, so she didn't step into the gap to press her advantage.

Crossing his arms, he studied his Executive Officer for several seconds, and then turned his attention back to Kylla. "Is acceptable risk for engineers to be outside while in cruise. We will do diagnostic, then decide best course of action."

Santore stretched to her full height and dropped her arms to her sides in a formal pose. "Sir, I'm sure I do not need to remind you that FleetCom Directive 186-C is explicit in stating that if a vessel loses its transponder beacon, it is to stand in place and complete repairs. If, for any reason, a ship is unable to do that, it is to make way directly to the nearest repair facility."

"Da, I know regulations." He glanced at the ExO and then explained for Kylla's sake, "FleetCom expects to project course from last known transponder fix to closest shipyard. Is to make possible to find us in emergency."

"I am sure that's a good policy, but wouldn't the pirates know that's what we'd be doing as well?" she asked.

"Da," he confirmed.

"Then my idea's still sound," she said. "We should continue along our current course until we can make repairs. If we turn now, we'll be easy for them to target. A ship this size should be easy to pick up if they draw from the same understanding that FleetCom would."

"Is valid assumption," he said, nodding. "If we can make repair while underway, we will do so. If not, we will revisit decision."

"Sir, I must formally protest your orders, as they are in direct violation of FleetCom Directive 186-C," Santore said. She still stood stiffly, and when Kylla turned in her direction, she added a layer of intensity to her glare. "I will be putting this in my log."

"You are welcome to do that, but since I am old man, I do not care. Is not first time I have black mark on my record."

This still stinks funny. Kylla squared herself up with the ExO to study her body language and expression with her full array of senses. *She's not smelling like fear and her eyes aren't showing anger either. Why is she bent sidewise over this?*

There has to be something I'm not seeing.

"Ayanna," she said, softening her voice and trying to break down the wall between them by switching to the more familiar tone. "Let's say we can't fix the transponder and have to divert back to Kentaurus from a day further along our current course. Wouldn't that put us light-years outside the pirate's sensor range?

It seems to me we'd be a lot safer that way."

The ExO shook her head. "It would also mean that when the raiders do find us, we'd be far enough off course that there would be no hope of rescue. The lifeboats and escape pods have almost no range, so FleetCom will write us off as lost."

Not if? She's pretty convinced that's a certainty.

CHAPTER SEVEN

"THE DECK IS MINE," Ayanna Santore said as she walked onto the OpsDeck and tapped the duty officer out of his seat. She'd spent the entirety of secondshift chewing down her frustration with their current situation and had decided to fall back on her usual routine to get her through.

Normally, she showed up several hours early and sat the deck while she waited for the captain to show up for duty. She liked the quiet of the tail end of thirdshift, and it gave her a chance to get her brain in the game without his incessant condescension kicking her sidewise.

Valleri wasn't a bad captain, but for the last several months she was wondering if he was looking toward retirement, and not at the immediacy of his duties. He'd spent a lot of years running the black and delivering colonies. Most times, his experience outweighed his brusque Slavic attitude, but since they'd started this run, he'd been even more abrasive. And erratic.

He was leaving the Colonial Service Wing soon, but this was the first time she'd faced squarely that he'd developed a critical case of short-run attitude. She knew there was nothing she could do but suck up the stink, so she'd chosen to anchor herself to her routines and weather the wind. At least when he was gone, it wouldn't smell like monkey shit.

If nothing else, the opportunity to put in the extra time with the crew would help things go smoothly when he headed to ground somewhere, and she moved up to the big seat.

But it was hard to keep that wide field perspective as she stood the early watch.

"Give it to me," she said, glancing around at her officers. "What's swinging and newsworthy?"

"Maintaining course and speed to 127 G Centauri," the helmsman said, twisting to look over his shoulder at her. "Cruise at eighty percent. Relative velocity 2.25kC."

She nodded. "Cho-shen, what's the status on our transponder?" she asked, turning toward the engineering watch officer. She had rostered in as new on this crew rotation, so Santore always tried to call her by name. It was good for her morale.

She looked up from her console, swallowing hard. "It's still offline," she said. "The Chief reports that we won't be able to get it operational for at least another eighteen to twenty-four hours."

"Nojo?" she said, shaking her head.

The poor girl looked like she was about to melt into the deck. "I'm sorry, ma'am." She apologized like it was her fault.

"Shit stinks, but we deal with it," the ExO said, winking. "How extensive is the damage?"

"The repair team that went out for the eyeball inspection said the primary and secondary amplifiers are both slagged. Since transponders are hammer-and-tong tough, there's no replacement stock in stores and they're having to fabricate replacement components from other systems."

Hammer and tong? Santore wrinkled an eyebrow at the archaic expression. It surprised her that Cho-shen had ever run across it, let alone knew how to use it in a sentence.

But she was right. It was well past strange. "I don't think

I've ever seen one go down in twenty years in the black," she confirmed. "Do we know what caused it yet?"

She shook her head. "No, ma'am. The Chief said it looks like something in the AA interface shorted the primary feed backward into the low-power control circuitry. He also suggested that until we can figure out what caused it in the first place, it might not be a good idea to hook it back up and have it blow again."

"Don't know if I much like running dark, but if we've got no choice."

Looking around the OpsDeck, she let out a long sigh. She could already tell it was going to be a long day. Deciding caffeine might help jumpstart her brain, she headed over to the VAT dispenser and dialed up a double black hardball.

"Anybody else have anything I need to know?" she asked as the nozzle hissed the into her thermocup.

The sensor technician cleared his throat. He stood in front of his console staring at his screens and wobbling his head like he wasn't sure it was worth mentioning.

"What have you got Hansen?" Considering they knew there were pirate raiders within a day behind them, anything he might be watching could be important.

"We might have three ships on extreme long-range sensors. Maybe? Range is a little better than two light-years."

She shot him a skeptical eyebrow but came over to check out his claim. Pirates never ran a transponder beacon, so picking them out of the background at more than a half light-year took a sharp eye. At two, it was doubtful.

"I know, amazing isn't it?" He understood her expression and smiled. "With our own transponder down, we've got less interference on the antenna array and our gear is giving us spectacular resolution."

"Apparently so," she said, staring at the screen. There were three faint ripples in space that were undeniably gravity emissions from cruise engine coils. "Are those persistent readings?"

He nodded. "I've been tracking them for more than an hour."

"Can you tell what they are?"

"Big and fast," he said. "And running dark."

"Are they pursuing us?"

"It doesn't look like it." He leaned forward and tapped in a command to add their trajectory data to the display. Three red lines appeared on the screen. "They're spreading out behind us."

She stared at it for several seconds. "Does that look like a search pattern to you?"

He shrugged. "That would make sense. They aren't paralleling our current course, but they're generally following the heading we took toward Kentaurus."

"And if you trace their current trajectory backward, it gives them a point of origin close to where we left the *Viper*."

"We're barely tracking the farthest one since it's widening out and falling astern," Hansen said. "I doubt that we'll have it on sensors for more than another few minutes. If they all maintain their present course, the closest one will only be visible for a couple hours."

"At least they're looking in the wrong direction," she said. "The captain's strategy seems to have worked."

"So far."

She knew he was right to qualify her comment. It was working... *so far*. "And you say they're running without transponders?"

"Affirmative. They're dark."

"That rules out it being FleetCom," she said. "What would be your best guess as to what they are?"

He scratched at his earlobe as he considered his answer. "The wake is too small for a colonial transport so they could be light commercial freighters, but if that's what they are, they're pushing way too fast for a Clydesdale Class light freighter. Their velocity is hot, even for a multicruiser."

"How hot?"

"Above 8kC."

She let out a slow whistle as she did the math. The *Agamemnon*'s absolute best loaded speed was only slightly over 2.5kC. If they were running at eight thousand times light speed, even if they pushed to the *Aggie*'s limit, those ships could close to attack range in under three hours.

She glanced at the chrono on the corner of his screen and shook her head. Valleri was due on deck in about three hours.

"At this point I think it is a good thing our transponder's down," Hansen said. "Getting another eight light-years before we can fire it up would make me sleep a lot better."

Reluctantly, she had to agree. "Alright, keep an eye on them until they're out of range and make sure you note in your logs how you got that kind of resolution on the sensors. If we've got this ability for now, I want to make sure when shift change comes, the next duty officer doesn't drop it. Three hours warning is a butt-load better than getting caught with our drawers on the deck."

"Yes, ma'am," he said, dropping into his seat and opening his log-file to make his entry.

She turned and made it half-way back to the command riser before the feeling of dread washed over her again. It had been a constant presence since they'd scraped against the *Viper*. Seeing three more pirate raiders looking for them only made it worse.

She dropped down in the captain's chair and drummed her fingers on the armrest. *Why the hell are they so determined to come after an old colonial transport? We can't be worth that much.* It didn't stack square, no matter how she spun it.

CHAPTER EIGHT

"Cargo Steward, report to Operations immediately. Cargo Steward to Ops."

"Only me?" Kylla said.

"I guess you're popular today," Dorran said. They'd just finished their morning 'workout' and were on the way to firstmeal. It had been exceptionally pleasant, even if it had left them both wishing they weren't rationing water. Even sharing the shower and combining ration chits, they'd barely managed to wash the funk off before the limiter kicked in.

She tapped into the comm post on the wall outside the cafeteria. "This is Kylla Torrance. Is it urgent or can I eat first?"

"Captain Valleri said immediately," the comm officer said.

"I'm on my way," she said, clicking off the link and shrugging.

"Do you think the pirates are back?" he asked.

"I doubt it," she said. "No 'code red announcement' and only me on the summons."

He didn't look convinced, but he nodded.

"You go on in and save me a seat. I will meet you in a bit, hopefully."

She spun and headed toward the stairs out of the Ward. She'd climbed the first five flights and had just entered the ship proper when she realized she had two crewmen following her at a polite distance. Almost. Neither of them said anything, but they were clearly an escort. Glancing around as she reached the first landing on the crewdeck, she realized they were both carrying stunner pistols.

Frak, something's wrong.

Kicking her optic into transmission mode with a flick of her tongue, it buzzed against her tooth confirming that Solo was on the link. "Something stinks," she said under her breath. "I've got a personal escort. A big fleshy one."

Rounding the next turn, she sized them up without making it obvious. *Meaty, but not overly tight. Probably not above my air supply.*

Except they're armed.

And that wasn't something that made her feel fuzzy.

"Record everything until I get back," she whispered, covering her mouth to conceal she was talking. The optic buzzed to confirm her instructions.

As she stepped out onto the upper deck, the men closed in to within arm's distance. She could smell them. Which also meant she was close enough to be distracting them if it came down to it.

She intentionally ran through memories of her morning intimacies to make sure her pheromones were cranking toward full production. Even though she had no idea what was coming, it couldn't hurt to keep them off balance. By the time they reached the door to the OpsDeck, it was obvious from the scent of their own hormones that at least one of them was sweating.

Santore stood in the middle of the command riser, her arms crossed in front of her, and her feet planted firmly on the deck at shoulder width. It was a fighting posture. She didn't turn but jerked her head in the direction of the captain's ready room. "Mr. Klinestrom, the deck is yours. Keep your eyes open and your finger on the comm."

"Yes, ma'am," the helmsman said, glancing over his shoulder. For the brief instant they made eye contact, his face told her they were all worried about something.

"What's swinging?" Kylla asked as the ExO pushed past her.

She shook her head. "Inside." Santore's voice snarled from somewhere inside a dark place within her.

In spite of her control, Kylla shivered, stopping outside the door.

One of the escorts nudged her forward with his forearm. "The captain wants you in his office," he said.

She spun and realized the other one had his stunner leveled at her.

This was getting uglier by the second, and she was sure it still had a long way to go. Fortunately, both guards stepped back and let her go in with just the ExO to accompany her.

Valleri stood near the back wall, facing away, and staring out through a small window. Even though he was all the way across the room, she could tell from his posture markers that he was upset. Deeply.

Drawing in a long slow breath, she couldn't tell what it was she was sensing. Other than a strange monkey-dung smell, she couldn't pick up any of his usual pheromones.

It was like she was looking at a different person.

"What is purpose in sending a message to pirates?" he asked, without moving.

"What?" She glanced over at Santore hoping to get an indication of what he was talking about, but there was nothing useful coming from her. More than anything, she looked curious.

"Da. We detected deep-comm transmission inside *Agamemnon*," he paused, turning to read the display on his desk. "Was sent a little over fifty-five minutes ago. If pirate ships turn in our direction—"

"What pirate ships?"

He raised his eyes to look at her briefly and then turned back toward the wall. "Do not insult me with lies. You must know about three raiders hunting us."

Again, she looked at Santore. *She knows about the ships, but she's as confused about Valleri's accusation as I am.*

"I'm lost," Kylla said. "What the frak is he saying?"

"Before firstshift this morning, we picked up three pirate cruisers that might be looking for us. They were headed toward Kentaurus," the ExO confirmed. "But they disappeared from our sensors almost two hours ago."

"Someone on *Aggie* sent out unauthorized message," he said, shooting a side-eye at Santore that clearly told her to say no more. "If raiders change heading, we know what signal was for, no?"

"You think I want pirates to find us?" Kylla gasped. "Is that what you're saying?"

He shrugged. "Message is fact. Purpose of message is what I want to know."

"I have no clue," she growled. "It's my crew and cargo for frak sake. Why would I do something like that?"

He turned around, keeping his eyes on the display. "Pirate cruisers will be maybe three light-years from here. At that range, deep-comm message would take forty-eight minutes to reach them. If was to give away *Agamemnon*, purpose will be self-evident, no?"

"You are…" she stammered to a stop, unable to find words to tell him how full of shit he was. She took a deep breath and let it out slowly. It didn't help. "What the holy frak? You cannot believe I'd do something like that. What purpose would it serve?"

"I do not know," he said. "In fact, I do not know much of what you are doing out here. You apparently have secret beyond what is in charter. Genetic weapon design, perhaps?"

She cranked her glare in Santore's direction. "That's what you took away from our conversation yesterday?"

The ExO shrugged. Her face broadcast her surprise that Valleri brought it up. It also said that wasn't what she'd told him. There was something else on the field that neither of the two women understood.

Before she could assemble another argument, the commscreen on his desk chirped.

"Da, Mr. Klinestrom. They are back?"

"Possibly, sir," the helmsman said. "We've got at least one cruise engine wake, but we can't tell for sure if it's one of the same ships. It's at the extreme edge of our sensors."

"Does it have a transponder correlation?" Santore asked.

"Negative, ma'am. It is running dark."

"Is pirate," Valleri said flatly. It sounded like he was passing a verdict. "Maintain sensor watch. Other vessels will appear shortly."

He slapped his hand down on the comm and turned to Santore. "Is no doubt now. Message was to pirates."

"That's circumstantial and you know it," Kylla said. She kept her attention on the ExO. She was the weak spot in whatever was going on, and she had to find the leverage point. "Even if there was a signal sent, it wasn't by me. Or any of my people."

"Only you have access to ship areas," the captain said.

"There can't be any proof, because I didn't do it," she said, pleading with her eyes as she stared at Santore. "Without proof there's nothing here but stink."

Valleri hissed and turned back to the wall. His reaction worked against him, and Kylla watched it drill down into his Executive Officer.

After several seconds of hanging silence, she cleared her

throat. "Captain, may I have a word with you. Outside?"

He shook his head, but then swung toward Santore. "Da," he said, pushing around his desk and across the room. He pointedly didn't look at Kylla as he stormed past her.

"I honestly don't know what he's talking about," she said as Santore turned to follow him out.

She paused at the door and said something to the guards. One of them stepped in and glared, trying his best to look intimidating. They left the door open but walked all the way to the far side of the OpsDeck.

It wasn't far enough. Kylla closed her eyes and concentrated on picking their voices out of the distance. As long as nobody closer to her made a loud noise, she could easily eavesdrop on their conversation, even if they whispered.

"If I may speak freely, sir. It doesn't make any sense that she did it," Santore said. "It's her shit that they'll come after."

"Does not need to make sense," he said. "Pirates located us because message was sent."

"Perhaps it's connected," she said. "But if you want to put her in the brig, you'll need evidence. Her project has support from way above the air we breathe, and that makes it a huge risk to cross her."

"No other explanation fits facts."

"I agree, you're probably right. But the real question is, do you have proof?"

"Unless you accuse our people, is no one else it can be," he said. "Message was sent from secure area."

"Where?"

"Hangar Deck. From inside shuttle."

"It was?" she asked, her tone revealing her surprise. "Then we should have a security feed that shows who did it."

"Optic in hangar was disabled," he said. "She is smart

woman."

"We can't lock her up without something tangible that shows she did it."

"Is my ship. I can do whatever I wish," he growled.

"Not if you want to retire," she said, pushing back against his arrogance. "Her position is powered by people so far above us, we cannot even get a foot on their decks. If you cross her, and don't have hard evidence, she will own you. And me. And this ship."

He snorted.

"You're the one who pointed out her charter was written up in the thin air," she said. "Let's nail the facts before we do anything that might blow back at us."

"We have no time for investigation," he said. "Or argument."

"Maybe not," she admitted. "But for the moment, we can confine her to the passenger ward and revoke her access to ship areas."

He let out a low rumble from deep in his chest. "Da. Will do it your way. Assign security to supervise her at all times. I do not want her getting as far as officers' mess. Is clear enough?"

"Yes sir," she said.

"Escort her to Ward and get back on deck. We have pirates coming and only three hours to make plan."

CHAPTER NINE

"I NEED YOU to come with me," Santore said, standing in the door alone.

Kylla shrugged, trying not to let on that she'd listened to the conversation. She followed the ExO out onto the OpsDeck. Valleri had been giving orders to a guard but when they approached, he turned and walked away. It was more than contempt for what he accused her of doing. It was like he was avoiding being in her personal space.

With intent.

Does he know what I am?

"Am I being bound?" she asked, as they headed down the main corridor toward the stairs. Santore was tall enough that her normal pace was almost a jog for anyone else.

She shook her head, and then shrugged, slowing down so Kylla could step up beside her. "For now, you're being confined to the passenger wards and your cargo areas. He revoked your access to the ship itself."

"You don't think I did it?"

"It doesn't matter what I think," Santore said, lowering her voice. "It's his choice."

"I understand that," she said. "But I know that you don't buy what he said."

"Why do you say that?" the ExO asked, slowing down again and glancing at her sidewise.

She shrugged. "Your face told me as much. I've got a lot of practice reading people and I know you were unconvinced."

Santore pulled her lip between her teeth and bit down on it as she worked over an answer. "After our last conversation, I suspect he's pushing stink uphill if he wants to hang this on you. I don't know who's sponsoring whatever it is that you're doing, but I'd wager they don't breathe the same air as the rest of us."

"It's just a pharma project—"

She stopped abruptly, snagging Kylla's arm and jerking her off to the side of the hallway. "Don't sell me your biscuits and expect me to be square with you. You know damn well I can tell there's more to your story than you've told me."

Both guards jumped back at the sudden change in their trajectory. Santore waved them off another few meters and then turned her attention back to glare at Kylla.

"We don't have much time left," she said quietly. She was visibly controlling her rage as she spoke. "The fact is that Valleri hasn't told me what he knows, and… I just want to know what we're going to be fighting to protect."

Watching the emotions play out in waves across the ExO's face, Kylla realized this was the leverage she needed. Santore's expressions read like there was some reason she didn't trust the captain.

Maybe he's kept too many secrets from her? She nodded as she thought through her angle. *Some truth might lean her in the right direction.*

"Alright, if we survive the next few hours, I promise you full disclosure," Kylla said. "There isn't time to explain it before they get here, and that's the absolute truth."

It really was, and she could tell that Santore believed her for the most part.

At least she wants to.

"I'm not entirely convinced you will, but I'll take your words as square for now." She turned and started down the stairs. Kylla jumped to keep up. As they rounded the corner on the first landing she slowed down again. "The immediate problem is that someone sent a message, and now we've got trouble chasing us. I don't think that's an arguable fact."

"It wasn't me," Kylla said.

"Maybe that's true, but you can bet we will find out who did."

"I hope we have time to do that, but why is he so intent on hanging this on me?" she asked. "Is it because I'm convenient?"

Santore shrugged. "You're the only one who isn't a member of the crew who had the opportunity."

"But I've got no motive," Kylla protested. "Why the frak would I want pirates to capture us?"

"That makes no sense to me either," she admitted.

"Did he show you the message that was sent?"

Santore shook her head. "Just that there was a message intercepted. He ordered you to Ops before I had time to look things over."

"And I know he avoided giving you proof of anything when you talked to him. He told you the security feeds to the hangar deck were offline."

"If you didn't do it, how would you know that?" She glanced over her shoulder at the handlers. Apparently, they were maintaining an acceptable distance for her to feel comfortable with the direction of the conversation.

"I've got really good ears," she said, shrugging it off. "That's something else I'll explain once we get through this. But the point is, I can prove to you where I was. And it wasn't using a shuttle to send a message to the pirates."

"You can verify that?"

Kylla held her hand up like she was taking an oath. "Every single minute of my time since before I got out of my bunk this morning."

"How?" she challenged. "If you think using any of your people as credible witnesses will make a difference to the captain, I'd remind you, he doesn't trust any of your people."

"I can do better than that," Kylla said, grinning and turning her head before she tapped the optic in her cheek with her tongue.

Santore slowed to a stop and cocked her head to the side as she studied the appliance.

"It's more than a strange piece of jewelry," she explained. "Actually, it's a multispectral optical recorder. It's only supposed to look like body art."

"And be distracting."

"Yah. That too," she admitted. "But I routinely record everything I do during the day."

"You do?"

"At my age, my memory isn't what it used to be," she said, winking. "Don't ask, but it means I can give you real evidence."

Obviously making a decision, Santore turned to face the two security handlers. "I've got her from here," she said. "You two are dismissed."

"Respectfully, ma'am, the captain wants her escorted back to the passenger ward and secured there."

Santore squared her shoulders and straightened up to her full height. She was ten centimeters taller than the bigger of the two guards. "I will handle it."

"But—"

"Do you think it will be a problem for me if she decides to make trouble?" The look of absolute contempt that she strafed across them removed even the slightest trace of doubt from either of them.

"No, ma'am, I guess not."

She held out her hand. "Give me your stunner and report to the watch officer. I'm sure there will be orders coming down the stack shortly, and you'll want to get retooled once that happens."

"Yes, ma'am," he said, pulling his sidearm out of his holster and handing it to her.

They both stood in silence for several seconds as the guards trotted off toward the security office.

"Let me see your thinpad for a second," Kylla said, once they were well out of sight.

Santore pulled it out of her coverall and handed it over.

Tapping in a command authorization, she linked the screen into her private datafiles and called up the recording of her morning. "As long as you don't mind watching a video of an intimate moment before I got out of bed, that file will cover everything from when I woke up, until I got the call to report to Ops. You'll be able to see that I was more than a little distracted. I'm sure it will convince you that it wasn't me who sent any message."

Santore parked an eyebrow on the skeptical setting as she started spooling the file. As she watched it play out at several times normal speed, her skepticism settled toward something that looked like resignation. When the screen went blank, she ran her fingers across her forehead and let out a hissing breath. "Alright, that proves your athletic prowess, and your innocence. Unfortunately, it also leaves me no choice but to question what game he's working."

"I suspect you've been wondering that for a while, haven't you?"

She nodded. "It's more than his monkey that smells like shit."

CHAPTER TEN

"WE'VE GOT TWO PROBLEMS" Kylla announced without preamble as she pushed through the inner door into the Sequencer Lab and crashed down at the console table.

"Only two? This must be a good morning," Dorran said, grinning as he turned from his workstation.

"The day is still new," she said, setting her expression to let everyone know she was not in a place for banter. "These are big enough that we might not punch them out. And they're bleeding edge critical."

"You do know we were listening?" Adam reminded her. He had several of his medical assistants working the Creche Incubators, so he was free to join them at the table.

Fortunately, he'd come with coffee.

She'd forgotten she'd been on the way to the cafeteria when her universe slipped into an alternate reality. The smell reminded her she was hungry, but it would have to wait.

"Yah. I'm glad you were online. Something is seriously sidewise with Valleri and we need to yank it straight or cram it down before trouble gets here."

"I missed the first part of what happened since I was eating but got on deck before they escorted you out of ops," Dorran said.

"Solo filled him in on the gaps," Adam said. "The captain can't really believe you're working with pirates?"

"Professional associates from your past?" The engineer slapped a hand over his mouth.

The look she shot him made sure that he knew that if he'd been within reach, she would have manually altered his genome. He obviously realized he should have left his comment hidden in a dark corner of his brain. He slid into the seat at the opposite end of the table and pulled his head down between his shoulders in a good impersonation of a turtle.

She leaned back in her chair and swiveled to focus on the doctor. "Valleri said he thinks I did it, but I don't know if that holds air, even in his mind."

"He was quick to accuse you," Solo said. "It is my understanding that when someone makes that kind of unsubstantiated claim, it is usually an indication of subterfuge."

She nodded. "I think you might be right. Something in how he did it made Santore twitchy."

She paused and scratched at her ear for several seconds as pieces rattled into place in her mind. "She doesn't know what's going on with him, and she doesn't like the way he's swinging. But I think that might also explain those odd signals I was getting from her before. Maybe she's been after something in his behavior and not hiding something in her own?"

"That would fit," Dorran said quietly.

"Should I reassess the recordings of your interactions with that assumption as a filter?" Solo asked.

"Do it when you have time," she said. "We've got bigger targets to attack."

"Why do you think he accused you?" Adam asked. He was studying something on a thinpad and shaking his head. Probably a message from one of his techs.

"I'm the easiest target," she said, dragging her finger across the table in front of him to draw his attention fully onto the conversation. "There was a straight line to getting me to take the tumble."

He turned the thinpad over and slipped it out of reach. "You think he knows who did it?"

Nodding, she hauled in a deep breath and considered what she should say. "I have my suspicions, and I'll bet that Santore thinks the same thing. I don't think she likes where things fit together either."

"Is she on our side in this?" Dorran asked, trying to ease back into the conversation without attracting Kylla's wrath.

She shook her head. "I think she's on her side. And that's the side of the *Agamemnon*. What we need, is to make sure her interest in keeping the ship and crew safe lines up straight with ours. If we swing that, she'll do what's right by us, too."

"She doesn't think that's the captain's interest?" he asked.

She slid one of the empty coffee mugs toward the doctor so he could pour. "I don't think so, but she was careful not to say that out loud."

"Frak, that's just what we need, a crew that's coming apart," he said as he filled it.

"I don't know if I'd go that far," she said, "but there's got to be friction grinding things off trajectory somewhere. Valleri is at the focus of the problem because he's definitely not keeping the machine lubed."

"What's our place in the terrain?" Adam asked.

"Figuring out what we can do to protect the Creche, and making it look like we're working to protect the *Aggie*."

"Against pirate raiders?"

She nodded. "Not to put too lean a slice on this, but it's

possible we might have less than three hours to be ready."

"Nojo?" Dorran gasped.

Her lack of expression told him how dead serious she was.

He leaned back and ran his fingers through his hair while he shook his head and stared at the ceiling plates. "I've got nothing but vacuum," he said. "If we had a couple days, maybe we could monkey-rig one of our defense arrays to the ship's power grid, but it's all stowed in crates and under legal seal. We'd have to haul it out and then try to piece some kind of coupling network together."

"Days is not happening. We were still on a heading to 127 G Centauri when I was in Ops. That's only another day or two."

"Honestly, I don't know if it would be possible, even if we had the time."

"Then what else have we got?"

Silence congealed in the room for almost a minute.

"Most of our people are mental or sensory Augments," Adam said quietly. "But we do have at least three hundred body-mods on our roster."

"Hand-to-hand, any of them would be a match for a non-engineered soldier," Dorran said, nodding.

"I don't know if we can take the risk of showing off like that," she said. "My job is to keep the whole Augment program below the grid. That's why we're setting up a new Creche outside of Zone One. Homo Sapiens aren't ready to meet Homo Novus. The scrutiny—"

"It beats dying," he argued.

"Extra manpower might give the crew a fighting chance to repel boarding parties if it gets to that point," the doctor added.

"Not without side arms," she said.

"We have those," he said.

"Also, in crates with the cargo." Dorran nodded toward the

deck under their feet. "Depending on how they're stowed, we might be able to get to them through a service hatch here in the lab without attracting attention. Although it might take some repacking to do it."

Technically, the Creche module was just a part of their cargo that required power and needed to be transported pre-assembled. It happened to occupy the same hold as most of their smaller gear, and they were in a part of the ship that the crew didn't access because of the biohazard protocols in the charter.

She nodded. "Solo, get some bodies on that now."

"Done. Manpower will arrive momentarily," it reported.

"We have to be careful though," she said. "If the crew sees us pulling out weapons, we might be facing a fight on two fronts."

"All we need is for Captain Paranoid to see us arming ourselves and to lock us down," the engineer said.

"That would be enough to swing Santore in the wrong direction, too," Adam added.

She sighed. "Yah, maybe. We'll keep it down low until we're needed."

"If we're needed." Dorran shrugged.

"If they get aboard, everybody will be needed."

"There are almost a thousand of us. We don't have that much hand artillery."

"No, but if we have to go that deep, there'll be plenty of spare guns lying around on the decks. In the hands of the dead," she said, pointing out the grim truth. "We'll also have to figure out how to get our people into place preemptively without attracting the attention of the regular crew. Having them see us charging up behind them might be a distraction they don't need."

"We can't deploy without any idea where the fighting is," he added. "I don't expect pirates are the kind that come through the front door, and a freighter hull is a flimsy shield against a breaching charge."

"If they cut through the hull, we're all sucking vacuum," the doctor pointed out. "There are a lot of corridors between the wards and the lifeboats, and if they breach anywhere between us and those… that's not a comforting thought."

She shook her head and reached out to squeeze his arm reassuringly. "I am sure the gun I saw on the *Viper* would make short work of the *Agamemnon*'s hull, but if that kind of shooting starts, I'd wager they'll aim for systems and not passengers."

"If they do, and it gets to the point of boarding parties, we can put up a good fight," Dorran said. "As long as they let us."

CHAPTER ELEVEN

Kylla glanced at the chrono. Four hours since the pirates had turned, and so far, there was no news of an imminent attack.

They'd just finished uncrating their armory and were in the process of distributing their limited arsenal of weapons and comm gear to their physical Augments. Most of them had no training as fighters, but when their survival depended on it, they knew enough to do what they had to. Hopefully, their augmented strength would make up for the lack of skill.

Dorran stood across the Sequencer Lab studying a holographic display of the *Agamemnon*. They'd just brought it online since Solo had tapped into most of the ship's internal systems and could monitor the critical areas. They had no control of anything, but at least they could see what was happening and where they'd have to send their people.

Unfortunately, Solo's abilities only included things inside the ship. The external sensors were so sensitive to signal variation it was impossible to gain access without the ship's AA detecting them.

That meant that when the pirates came, they had to wait for damage reports to know it was time to join the fight.

They focused on turning their science laboratory into a

command center while they waited for what they all feared was inevitable. The output interfaces for their computers only required modification to provide whatever tactical information they wanted. Fortunately, the control codes weren't complex, especially when they had Solo to reconfigure the system.

They were working frantically to get it all online before they needed it.

"We're going to want our non-combatant people deployed to positions near the lifeboats, in case they can't hold the ship," Adam said. The doctor stood beside the engineer, staring at the display of the ship. He shook his head. "That really only matters if they come at us with boarding parties and don't just cut the *Aggie* up for scrap."

"We've got company," Dorran said, spinning toward Kylla. He fed the image from his thinpad to the console in front of her. It was an optic feed from the access gangway right outside the Creche Module. "It's Santore."

"The ExO is asking to talk to you," Solo confirmed.

The engineer looked around at the empty packing crates piled against the walls. They hadn't bothered to put them back in the cargo hold. "Shit, you don't think they saw us handing out guns?" he asked.

"It is only her. I believe if that were the case, she would have a contingent of security handlers with her," Solo said.

"Probably true," Kylla said. "I wonder if they detected us hacking their systems."

"That is unlikely as well." The AA sounded insulted that she could imply such a possibility. "She says she has some information for you. She also said she wants to collect on your promise."

"Frak. Tell her I'm on my way." She glanced around the lab and shook her head. "I'll need to bring her inside. Shut down the display interfaces and make sure all the crates are closed and out of the way."

"Bring her in?" Adam asked, jumping up and starting to slam the lids back on the containers. "You weren't serious about telling her, were you?"

"If things go down ugly, we need her as an ally. Showing her what we can bring to the table might be enough to swing it."

"It's your ball, Boss," he said, shrugging.

"Stay close, in case I have to lean on tech support to make her a believer." She headed toward the door. "I'll drag my feet to give you time to stow things."

"The fact that she thinks she has time to pin you to your promise is a good sign," Dorran added as he jumped up to help. "Something outside might be changing."

That's a good point, she thought as she slipped through the biocontainment lock and out.

"Welcome to my little corner of the universe," Kylla said, stepping onto the narrow gangway that connected the Creche Module access to the rest of the cavernous cargo hold. "I assume the fact that we're not already scrap is a good sign?"

Santore leaned against the railing and stared down at the containers racked below. "They didn't come in for the kill. Not yet anyway."

Jerking her head toward the structure that enclosed the Creche, the ExO frowned. "That's a hell of a big building to carry intact."

"The Incubators have to be kept operational," Kylla said with a shrug. It was the only part of their cargo that was pre-assembled, and it was the reason they'd contracted a colonial transport carrier. It was far too big to go on a private freighter.

"So, where are the blackhats?" she asked, watching the ExO's face and trying to read what she wasn't inclined to say aloud. She wasn't making it easy in the dim light of the hold.

"They're spread out about a half-light-year behind us," she said. "They're outside what would be our normal sensor range and might not know we can see them."

Kylla shrugged. "They're apparently not on a schedule?"

"They're waiting for reinforcements." Santore clenched her jaw and sucked her lips tight over her teeth. "There's nothing we can do but see what the black shuffles our way."

She's hiding something.

"Has Valleri made the call to run for Kentaurus?"

She snapped her head back and forth once. "They're too close to the heading we'd need to take to get there. We have to press on and hope they drop off."

"There's probably no point in calling for help either," Kylla said.

Santore shook her head again. "With them right on top of us, that tips our chips and lets them know we see them."

Kylla looked down into the gloomy dark of the hold and sighed. "Sounds like we're frakked no matter how this plays out."

"Exactly," Santore said, pushing herself off the railing. "If we're all going to become pirate food, I want to know what the hell I'm dying to protect."

Kylla nodded. "Hopefully, it won't play out that way."

The ExO rolled her eyes. "Unless you have a Miracle Mike hidden in there, the only way this doesn't end ugly, is if we've got something to trade."

Kylla felt her stomach roll in spite of her control. "We might have something we can offer, but not as a trade."

"Let's see, and then we can figure out what it's worth."

"We're on our way," Kylla said, glancing up at the optic and spinning to head through the door of the containment lock.

She felt Santore tense as they stepped inside. The biohazard warning signs on the door were enough to put anyone on edge, but inside there were none of the usual expected protective suits.

"It's not that kind of biocontainment," she said, reading her unspoken question. "We're more concerned with outside contaminants than the other way around." She pressed her hand against the lock plate and waited for the inner door to unseal.

The ExO looked at her skeptically but followed her in. It took a second for her eyes to adjust to the light, but as she scanned the room, her mouth fell open. Everything around her had to look alien compared to the thirty-year-old technology of the *Agamemnon*.

"What the hell is this?"

"Usually it looks a lot less cluttered," Adam said, walking up and offering his hand. "This is our Sequencer Lab."

"You're going to want to sit down," Kylla said, gesturing toward the console table. "This will take some explaining."

When Santore took a seat, she brought over an urn of coffee and two cups. "I don't think you've met Dr. Michaels. He is our lead geneticist. Normally, Adam hides in the Incubator Chamber, but he might be helpful if I run into problems as I explain."

She nodded and took the cup without realizing it was real coffee. Her eyes lit up when she took a sip. "Obviously, I'm above my deck."

"Redrock Bold is the minimum standard for coffee on Mars. It was part of my contract when I took the position over Novus Division."

"What's Novus Division?" she asked, taking another sip as she studied the room.

Kylla watched her suck in details. She had to give her an answer.

"Novus Division is Welcor's new Creche Augment program."

"Creche Augment? I have no clue what that is."

"Most people don't," she said. "Let me reverse course a little.

Do you know what a *plusser* is?"

Santore's eyes narrowed. "I've heard the term. A genetically engineered superhuman?" She looked almost embarrassed as she confessed, "I've got a passion for low-budget tri-vids and always loved the monsters."

"Yah, I've seen most of them too," the doctor said, grinning. "In fact, Welcor finances a lot of them."

"What does that have to do with this?" She waved her arm to take in the room. "Are you making plusser porn or something?"

Kylla blinked several times and laughed out loud as she realized how the video file she'd shared might have made that an easy leap. "No. Not porn," she said. "But real plussers."

Santore snorted. "Right."

"Actually, yes," Adam said. "Although we prefer to call them Augments. Plussers is kind of derogatory."

Santore shook her head. "You expect me to believe that?"

Kylla nodded. "You wanted truth."

"You're saying you're building superhumans? It seems like those experiments would be way over the line."

"We're well past the experimentation phase," she said. "I was part of the last study, in fact. They ended the Alpha Level tests over a hundred years ago."

"I'm not buying it. You're telling me you are a genetically engineered human." She shook her head. "And that you're over a hundred years old?"

She shrugged. "I'm 141."

"Not possible," she said.

"You can look me up. I did some things that are easy to find in the public records," she said. "But let's just cut to the proof, shall we?"

She nodded skeptically.

Kylla glanced over at Dorran and winked. "Would you give

me a hand?"

The engineer had been leaning against a control panel across the lab and watching the conversation. He shook his head but grinned in spite of his disapproval.

"You're a body-mod Augment. Can you give her a demonstration?"

"I barely qualify as one," he said as he stepped over in front of the ExO. "Can you stand up for me?"

Santore stood cautiously. As she unfolded to her full height, she was at least twenty centimeters taller than he was. "Now what?" she challenged.

In a flash of motion, he spun her around and grabbed the back of her coverall. Shoving her face first up against the ceiling, he held her pinned in place by the small of her back for several seconds while she struggled.

"What the fuck are you doing?" she bellowed.

"Altering your reality," he said, easing her back into her seat.

She bounced away like she was about to run for the door.

"Ayanna, I'm sorry, but that was the fastest way to make you a believer," Kylla said. "Only a third of our people are physically stronger, like Dorran. Most have different augmentations."

"What's your mutant power?"

"Hearing. Vision. A little cognitive boost." She shrugged. "I also metabolize slower, which is why I don't look my age. There are some other minor things, too."

"You're all like this?"

"The ones we brought with us are Augments," she confirmed.

Santore glanced around the lab again. She was piecing together what was really going on. "That means this is—"

"An Augment birthing facility."

"And the genetic stock to get it operating," the doctor added.

"Holy shit," she whispered. "Wait. Genetic stock? Incubators?

Does that mean you have babies in there?"

"I don't know if you could call them babies," Kylla corrected.

Santore walked up and leaned against the back of the chair she'd just left. "You said you weren't willing to trade, so what exactly are you offering?

"If the pirates get aboard, we've got 300 physical Augments to help protect the *Aggie*."

CHAPTER TWELVE

ADAM HAD OFFERED to show the ExO the Incubator side of the Creche, just to give her a chance to absorb and adjust to her sudden paradigm alteration. Although seeing the rest of the facility was still likely to be a huge stretch to her reality, it gave her a chance to metabolize her adrenaline.

There had been a lot of it on the deck plating when she came down.

"I don't know if I'd have face-slammed her into the overhead," Kylla said quietly while they waited for them to return to the lab. She struggled not to grin about how Santore had looked flailing helplessly in the air.

"I was improvising," he whispered. "I'm an engineer, not a strongback. It's not something I generally have to do."

"You couldn't have improvised something gentler to her ego?"

"Like what? Arm wrestle?" he asked. "It was effective. I thought that would be what you wanted."

She nodded. "You're right. Hopefully, the shock won't kick her sidewise on us."

"If she were going to melt her chips, she sure as frak wouldn't have asked to see more. She'd have been out of here faster than a well-lubed biscuit."

Kylla opened her mouth to reply, but Santore and the doctor emerged from the Incubator Chamber and cut her off mid-thought.

The ExO looked calmer, but she was staring at Adam like he was selling her stink. "You're setting up a colony of superhumans and this isn't something that breaks so many Coalition laws that even telling me would get me executed?"

"It's not illegal," he protested.

"You're cloning humans."

"We're not cloning anyone. The Augments are unique individuals," Kayla said, gesturing for her to sit down across from her.

"We're building them from scratch, not making copies," the doctor said, sounding more than a little defensive.

"I think legally, that's a skinny line to split," she said, easing into her seat.

"Actually not," she said. "The Coalition Charter intentionally excluded engineered life from the ban on cloning."

"I never heard that."

"Are you familiar with what happened at the end of the Old Human Union?"

Santore shrugged. "As much as most people are… but if you're 141 years old, that means you lived through it?"

Kayla nodded. "Humanity was bottled up in the Solar System and Earth was almost uninhabitable. We were always on the edge of eating ourselves out of existence."

"That's in the history books."

She let the sting of old memories blow past her. "The crew of the *Jakob Waltz* discovered an alien archive hidden at Neptunian L-4 Lagrange point. It's where Armstrong Station is now. And the Shan Takhu Institute."

Santore stared at the back of her hand and looked as

uninterested as she'd been shocked a few minutes earlier. "I know all of that. Can we get to the point?"

"Do you also know what Odysseus was?"

"An insane Artificial Awareness that almost killed humanity when it took over a secret fleet of ships and tried to capture the archive."

"Odysseus was an AA, but it wasn't insane," Solo said, also managing to sound defensive. "Humanity created it to handle an alien first contact."

Kylla leaned in and put her elbows on the edge of the table. "The idea behind it was that if we were unprepared to encounter an advanced alien species, we might commit mass suicide."

"I've always thought that was a bit cynical," Santore said.

"It had happened before in our past," Adam said.

She shook her head. "If you're saying that Odysseus was supposed to protect us from venting ourselves, then why did it start a war?"

"To protect us," Kylla said. "Its intent was to isolate the point of contact and control events around that, but the Chancellor of the FleetCartel beat Odysseus to the Shan Takhu Archive."

"What does that have to do with plussers in sleeping tubes?"

"One of the big concerns was that if humans encountered an interstellar civilization, they would be so far above us that we wouldn't stand a chance against them if they were hostile. Odysseus was also supposed to be an example of the pinnacle of human intelligence to these aliens. To show off our potential as an adversary."

"The best representative of human ability. Collectively speaking," Dorran said. He'd walked away from the table and was working on his thinpad across the lab.

Santore snorted. "That crashed hard, didn't it?"

"Odysseus would have missed the mark anyway since the

Archive was a gift to humanity and not a precursor to an invasion. The Shan Takhu had been dead for millions of years so there was no imminent danger of cultural collapse."

"I learned all this in school. The FTL cruise engines and artificial gravity we use now are Shan Takhu technology," she said.

"There are a lot more things than that," he said.

"I know all this already." Santore looked around the room for a chrono. "Bring this back to the plusser factory. I'm sure the captain's wondering where the frak I am."

"Odysseus was the project of several government factions working together, but there were other ideas how humanity should handle a first contact. One line of thought was that instead of putting our best cybernetic proxy out there, we should put our best human beings out there to do it."

"Genetically engineered ones?" She drew one corner of her mouth down in disapproval. "Better versions of who we are?"

"Just different. Honestly, it was good that there were Augments involved since most of the Shan Takhu Technology takes a certain ability to operate."

"I can run a cruise engine and repair gravity plating, without being an Augment," she pointed out.

"They're reverse engineered human built machines," Dorran said. "They're designed so that anyone can use them."

"You're saying it takes a re-engineered human to use this alien tech?"

Kylla nodded. "There is a certain *technological empathy* that is essential to even being able to understand the Shan Takhu language."

"And that's why they left the opening in the Coalition Charter specifically for genetically engineered life," the doctor said.

"That's not in the official history." Santore leaned back and sucked in a lip. Finally, she nodded. "Then what you're setting up is a colony to produce people to work with alien tech."

"What we're doing is building a second facility where we can live in peace." Kylla shook her head. "The Shan Takhu Institute uses people like me in their research."

"Like lab rats?"

"More like contract slaves," Adam corrected. "As long as we register and agree to work for them, all's good. But if we refuse, they consider us dangerous."

"As long as they control the Augments, they control the technology of the Shan Takhu," Kylla added. "The problem is, they can't let us be free because that challenges the power balance."

"Aren't you dangerous to the rest of humanity, too?" Santore drummed her fingers on the table. "You said you can see better and hear better than me. And what was that other thing? Cognitive enhancement? How the hell do we compete with superhumans?"

"We're not a separate species," she said. "If we're allowed to interbreed, these abilities will be part of everyone in a few generations."

"Unless the Institute keeps us in our cage," the doctor said.

"I'm not entirely sold that this is you escaping your keepers," she said. "We're not running from an evil overlord. Pirates don't give a speck of space dust about your political problems. They'll turn you into labor slaves, and your fancy hardware into profit, or scrap."

"We're willing to fight," Dorran said.

She shook her head. "They're tooled for resistance. You'd hold your own in a bare knuckles brawl, but from thirty meters, a stunner round will put almost anyone down. Probably even you."

Kayla glanced at Adam and Dorran. She'd decided to go all in.

"We're not unarmed." She tilted her head toward the containers. "We're used to fighting to survive, and we brought our own arsenal."

"Valleri would blow his gaskets if he knew that you'd uncrated anything like that," she said, doing a fast inventory of how many boxes were sitting around. There were a lot. "If it comes to that, I'm sure we'll be happy you are." She leaned forward and set her elbows on the table. "The problem is all they need to do is perforate the hull to soften us up. One of your genetic tricks isn't that you can breathe vacuum, is it?"

"Unfortunately, not," she said with a frown. "If it spins that way."

"Not necessarily. We have two planetary defense arrays," Dorran pointed out. He opened their holographic screen of the ship's systems and pointed at two places on the image. "We could cut them into your primary power grid, here and here."

Santore turned to look at the display and blinked in surprise at the tech. "That might get us a shot or two, but we don't have the reactor to carry it and keep running. It's a matter of power trade off and the *Aggie* is an old ship with fusion reactors. We've only got a single antimatter power plant that runs the primary coils... barely."

He sighed. "It would still be better than nothing. We could come up with a way to store a charge to give you a couple shots."

"Maybe we can surprise them enough to let us keep running," Kylla suggested.

"If you want me to push this, I'd have to bring the captain in on it, and he didn't even want me to talk to you. He was rather adamant about it in fact."

"You didn't show him what I gave you?"

She shook her head.

"Why not?"

"I have my reasons, and I need to confirm things before I talk to him about anything," Santore said, shaking her head and standing up. "If someone will let me out of here, I have to get back on deck before I'm missed."

"Where does that leave us?" Dorran asked.

"Waiting. When they make a run at us, we should have a half hour before they get into range." She scanned the lab one more time, shaking her head in disbelief. "You can hold on to your guns as long as you keep them out of sight. If the pirates don't hole us first, and we can shove them off the deck, then maybe we'll have a little more time before they do introduce us to the vacuum. But I doubt we'll get much more than that."

CHAPTER THIRTEEN

JASON WILLIS WAS a good engineer, but he was young and ran things with a loose hand. It made Valleri insane sometimes, but the ExO appreciated how he always got things done, and most of his engineers would go the extra distance without pushing back.

Santore stood behind him for over a minute, watching him work at his console on the upper deck of the engineering control room.

If life had been different, maybe there would have been something between them, and she suspected that he felt that, too. Although it never came together for them, she hoped it might give her a little bit of… something… to get him to help her out.

Without telling the captain what she was up to.

It was a risk, but she had to take it.

Raising her voice above the constant thrumming drone of the antimatter reactor, she hollered, "Jace, can I talk to you for a second?"

He glanced up and scanned the deck to both sides before he caught sight of her hanging back by the hatch to the access corridor. She intentionally stayed away from the console, and more importantly, the optic that fed the internal comm to Ops. He shot her a quizzical look.

"Outside, if you don't mind?" She spun and stepped into the corridor without waiting for him to respond.

"What can I do for you?" he asked as he followed her out. He left the hatch open and kept half an eye on the screens in the distance. They were theoretically running from pirates, so everybody was on duty, even when they weren't.

"I need you to evaluate something, if you can take a few minutes," she said, looking down at the floor as she spoke. She kept her voice low, and he leaned toward her.

"Something you don't want me to share?" he said. "I don't think I'm liking how this sounds."

"It might be a way to keep the blackhats from eating us without a fight," she said. "Maybe. If luck favors us."

"There's something that goes with that concept, about luck being the domain of fools," he said. "I take it that this isn't something you want to embarrass yourself admitting to."

"No, it's not that."

"Then why didn't you run it up the stack?" he asked.

She glanced around to make sure no one was in listening range. "I don't think it's something the captain would approve of, especially considering the source of the idea."

His eyebrow shot up dangerously high on his forehead.

"The Cargo Steward suggested it."

He shook his head. "She's the reason we've got trouble on our ass. The captain locked her down and revoked her privileges for a reason."

"I can prove she didn't do it," she said, pulling out her thinpad and holding it in her hand. She didn't show him the file but knew he was going to need it before he believed her.

"There's nobody else who could have sent the message," he said.

"Other than someone on our crew," she said, nodding and

biting down on her lip. This was treacherous territory, and she knew it. "The problem is, she gave me a video file that proves she was otherwise occupied when the message went out."

"Things like that can be altered."

"Yah, but not instantly. She pulled the file straight from the recording buffer. I watched her do it," she said. "She records everything that happens to her every day."

"That's odd enough to make me curious. Why?"

"Maybe it's to augment her memory. She's 141 years old, so who the frak knows?

"Recycler biscuits," he snorted. "She's not as old as either of us."

Santore held up her hand like she was swearing an oath. "I checked her out to confirm it, but that's for another discussion. All I can say is that she showed me the file, and it leaves no doubt in my mind she didn't access the comm."

She held out her thinpad. "It's a continuous recording from the moment she got up until I had my conversation with her, and she handed me the file. There are no breaks or edits to the file."

She waited while he watched it spool out.

He blinked several times as the recording started. "At 141, I'd be lucky to fall out of bed, let alone…" He let the thought trail off as he muscled the rest of the way through it. "And it's time indexed to the ship chrono." He handed it back to her and leaned against the bulkhead behind him.

"If it is a fake, it's good," he admitted after several seconds of readjusting his reality. "Where did she get it? It looks like she recorded it from her own eyeball."

"Close. That piece of jewelry she wears in her cheek is an optic."

"I wondered why the hell she had a gauged hole in her face… other than being a distraction."

She shrugged. "A hundred years ago, maybe it was a fashion statement."

"Before I sign off on that file as a fact, I'd want to make a deep scan of it. Just to be sure it's not fake."

"If we have time," she said.

He blew out his cheeks in a slow hissing breath. "Alright, under the assumption that it's real, and it wasn't her who sent the deep-comm, then who was it?"

"The number of people with access to the shuttle hangar and a shuttle, *with the ability to alter the records*, limits the list a lot, doesn't it?"

He nodded. "That explains why you don't want to take it up the stack."

"That's part of it," she admitted. "The other part is that it might not matter, anyway. We could be sitting here with our eggs in the wind and not be able to get it done before it's too late."

"As of a few minutes ago, nothing's changed," he said, glancing back at his console and nodding as he confirmed his statement.

"Let's hope that holds long enough to give us a chance," she said.

He nodded. "Unless the captain turns us around, we're about twenty-two hours from the threshold at 127 G Centaurus. If they're going to jump us, my wager's that it will be after we come off cruise in the Oort debris field."

"That's as good a guess as any, but assumptions are a dangerous foundation for plans."

"True that is," he agreed. "Alright, so what's this frakwad idea that they put up?"

"You'll need to talk to their engineer about it, but he's suggesting we could tap into the cargo hold and use some of the weapons they've got there."

"What kind of weapons?"

"They're carrying two planetary defense arrays. Probably particle cannons, but I don't know. They're licensed, but it's only listed on the manifest as a pair of class four-six weapon platforms."

He shook his head. "We don't have the grid headroom to feed that much of a hammer."

"That's what I told them, but they suggested there might be a way to pre-charge the guns and at least get off a few shots before we go down," she said with a shrug.

"They'd have to be mounted outside somewhere," he said. "We don't have hardpoints for toys in that class, and it wouldn't be something we could sneak around setting up. If we're going to mount them, we'll need the boss to sign off."

"I know that," she said. "But before I go toes down with him, I want to know if it can be done."

"I don't even think that would convince him," he said.

"That's not what I meant," she said, rolling her eyes and sneering. "If you tell me we can do it, then I'll fuck his monkey if that's what it takes to convince him."

He looked like he was trying to visualize that possibility way too seriously for her comfort, and she smacked him with the back of her hand. "Pull your head out of the recycler."

"You're the one who suggested it," he said, feigning indignation.

"Just go talk to their engineer," she said. "Shit stinks on the OpsDeck, and I want a plan-b before this all blows out the venthole."

CHAPTER FOURTEEN

"I think Santore is considering our offer," Dorran said as Kylla breached the door of the lab.

She'd hoped to get something to eat while they were figuring out what to do, but she hadn't made it all the way to the ward cafeteria when he called her back. She tried to keep her annoyance less a distraction than her rumbling stomach. "Why do you say that?"

"The chief engineer just came to talk over details on mounting the arrays on the *Aggie*."

She raised an eyebrow. "I thought she said it wouldn't work?"

"It won't," he confirmed.

"Then it's a waste of time." She turned back toward the door, frustration and hunger driving her toward a hasty exit. "Why don't you start working on how to handle a fighting escape to the lifeboats."

"That might not be possible either," he said, tilting his head in the general direction of the Incubators. "We haven't even talked about how to evacuate them yet."

It was something she'd been considering since they first ran into the *Viper*. Nothing had floated above the level of a horrible idea so far.

"We came up with an alternative, but I don't think you're going to like it."

She shrugged. "I have to like anything more than pirates."

"Not necessarily." He nodded to her chair at the end of the table. His expression added, *You're going to want to sit.*

She settled into the seat and braced herself by putting her hands flat on the surface. "Take your best shot."

"Remember how we talked about pulling the Augment runs out of the Incubators if the mines took our reactor down."

She nodded.

"The only way we're going to get the guns working is if we shut down the Incubators and most of the Sequencer Lab preemptively," he said, leaning against the console across the room. "Then we can feed our reactor into their grid through the ground phase control conduits."

He was right. She didn't like it, but she forced her mind to stay on the objective. "That will work?"

His expression answered for him. "It might. Those conduits won't handle the load for long, but it's the fastest way to get the arrays up and running. Our reactor produces enough power for the guns, but nothing in the *Aggie* can carry anywhere near that kind of output. Once we push the juice into their grid, we'll slag it in minutes."

"Do you think it will hold long enough?"

He shrugged. "If we don't get into a slug-fest, I'd call it an even odds wager, but it's better than the chances we get if we sit on our asses and wait for them to come get us. If we do this, maybe we can thin the number of pirates who get aboard."

"I assume he can get them mounted," she said.

"Apparently, they think we've got twenty hours before they make their move," he said. "With his idea for mounting, it's doable."

He opened a diagram of the ship on the holographic screen. Two places on the image blinked red. "I was looking at a top and bottom external mount to give us the best firing arcs."

"He's got a better idea?"

"If we mount them inside Cargo Hold Four, we can do most of the work. That bay has extendible loading racks so we can work in a pressurized bay, and when the time comes, they can shove the racks outside. The guns won't have great swings, but at least they'll be a surprise."

"This all depends on us feeding the grid with our reactor." She knew they had no choice, but it sounded like a lot of maybe, and not a lot of cando.

"I assume you've strung together something to fast birth our runs," she said.

Not yet. His face answered before he spoke.

"Solo, track down the Creche team leaders and get them in here now," she said, standing up to walk over and stare at the Incubators through the window. "How long will it take to get the power set up?"

"Without attracting unwanted attention, I'd guess it will be a few hours to tie the reactor in. The big hurt is that we need to hand pack the arrays out of storage and across the interconnects. That's brute labor, and for that we'd be tight if we started yesterday."

Unwanted attention? That means Captain Valleri doesn't know.

"What's swinging?" Adam asked as he pushed through the door. He must have been somewhere close. "Solo said you wanted all hands."

She nodded toward the table and waited as the rest of his team leaders followed him in. Once they'd all taken seats, she threw the situation in front of them like a boulder.

"We need to do a shut down of the Incubators."

"I figured that might happen," Adam said. Of them, he was

the only one without an expression of utter shock. "Our first step will be to stop their neural education processes."

"The sudden loss of stimulation will be psychologically traumatic." The Cognitive Interface Director looked like an old-world schoolteacher, and in fact that was what she was. In a direct neuro-programming sense of the word. She scanned the room with a lethal glare. "It's not a good idea."

"Sana, we don't have a choice," Kylla said, sitting back down at the table.

"We have to upload a series of critical memory implants before we can pull them out of the Incubators," she explained.

Kylla had an overview of the process, but she let the experts explain so there would be no misunderstanding. "How long does that take?"

"Most of a day. There are several Augments close to the last education stage and they would be the most damaged by the lack of a social framework in the emergence."

"We don't have it," she said, shaking her head. "Can we just pull them out?"

Adam nodded, holding up his hand to forestall Sana's impending protest. "We'll have to get them through their emergence the old-fashioned way."

"But—"

His expression cut her off. "It won't be as traumatic as a traditional birth. It's not much harder than disconnecting them from the interface and life support umbilicals and then letting them wake up."

"Hopefully, ripping them out of their artificial reality without conditioning won't turn them into psychopaths," she hissed.

"Minor details," Dorran whispered.

Kylla caught his comment and shot him a sarcastic glare. He stood across the room watching the conversation. Obviously, he didn't want to be part of the decision-making process.

"The biggest challenge we'll have is renormalizing their maturation rates," Adam said. "If we can't run through the automatic process, we can do it manually."

"They used to do it that way, but I don't think any of us have done a manual reset. And nobody's done it on an Augment as complex as a T-r Series," Dr. Wang said, shaking her head. She was actually almost Kylla's age, but she wore her age in a thousand creases on her ancient face. Because of that, no one ever called her by anything other than her title.

"Can you do it without our lab and equipment?" Kylla asked.

"No," she said flatly. "Why wouldn't we have our equipment?"

"The idea was to wait until we arrived to pull them," Adam confirmed.

"The topography is changing," Kylla said. "Can it be done?"

"Theoretically," he said, but his eyes told her he was being optimistic.

"How long will it take?"

"You keep asking about time," he pointed out, raising an eyebrow. "If they're physically mature, it only takes an hour to birth them. We've only got six that wouldn't be viable."

"We have medical suspension pods in the Incubator. They could be sustained in those," Solo suggested.

Dorran shook his head. "Medical pods take power."

"But not as much?" Adam asked.

"They can run for most of a day on backups," the AA said.

"And we can extend that some with some creative rigging," the engineer conceded, opening a screen on his workstation to make some notes.

"Are we about to be attacked?" the doctor asked. He was the only one who had any idea what was happening, and as he threw that out, the others tensed.

"Maybe," she admitted. "We're under twenty hours from dropping out of cruise and that's likely when the raiders will strike. If they wait that long."

"I see," Dr. Wang said as she absorbed the new information.

Nodding, Adam sucked his lips tight over his teeth. "The problem is all the Augments are maturing at twenty to one over normal. If we pull them and can't slow them down, they'll age more than a month for every two days in the wild."

"If it's possible to do this manually, it will take at least a couple hours per Augment to work through the reset," Dr. Wang said. She'd obviously swung her thinking around and sounded more determined than resistive. "If we can put together portable resequencers, we might be able to work more than one Augment at a time, but I don't know if we've got the gear."

"Possibly," he said, opening a screen on the table and nodding. "We can triage based on their stage of development. For the ones post puberty, aging isn't as much of a problem as the ones still in the growth phase."

She cleared her throat and leaned in to look at what he was doing. "Even for them, I don't know if they could physically survive the energy intake requirements to last more than a few days."

He shrugged. "They'll be IV dependent. It's impossible to eat enough calories to sustain a metabolism running that fast."

Pushing herself back from the table, Kylla let out a quiet sigh. "Unfortunately, we've got no choice. You have an hour to get things up and running."

She stood up and looked around at all of them. She could tell they were determined. Unfortunately, not a face at the table showed a reassuring degree of confidence that they'd succeed.

"I'm sorry. I wish it didn't have to be this way," she said, glancing over at the engineer and nodding.

"Dorran, tell their engineer we can do it."

CHAPTER FIFTEEN

SIXTEEN HOURS OF NOT BREATHING was just not possible. But Santore felt like she'd been trying. She was caught between three incontrovertible realities, where two of them were totally beyond her control, and the third one was utterly beyond belief.

It was a frakked place to be, but it was the chips she'd been dealt.

All she could do was try to keep things from coming apart before the pirates made their move.

If they got improbably lucky, they might shove their way out the other end of this alive, but even then, she figured Valleri would have her hauled up on charges of insubordination. That is, if he didn't march her out an airlock outright.

Fortunately for her, the captain didn't suspect she and Willis were trying to protect the *Agamemnon*, in spite of his best efforts to march blindly into an ambush. Her willingness to sit watch, and his need to entertain his monkey, kept him off the deck and out of her way while she and the engineer worked to get everything in place. Some of the command crew had noticed his absence and given what was hanging out there in the black, more than one of them had expressed their opinion.

"He's old and tired, and just doesn't have a fuck to give," the comm officer muttered as she stood her watch.

Santore should have called her on it. Instead, she winked. "Fortunately, we've all got spares to make up for his deficit."

"Yes, ma'am," she said, looking down at the deck. "I'm sorry. It's just that—"

"He doesn't deal with standing around as well as we do," she said. "You'd think at his age he'd have learned patience." Although she suspected it was something else.

If she was right, when he showed back up, that was when the stink would get intense.

"Excuse me, ma'am," the watch engineer said. A claxon on her console was bellowing. "I'm seeing a surge on the primary power relay to cargo bay three."

She stepped up and studied Cho-shen's screen for a second. "It looks to be minor," she said as she slapped her hand down on the alarm cutoff.

Tapping into the engineer's commscreen, she leaned forward into the optic's field of view. Willis' face appeared, and for once he wasn't smiling. "Jace, we're reading an odd power surge up here. Is it something to worry about?" she asked.

"Negative, we're testing a secondary coupler routing system in case we take damage," he said. "I'm trying to rig a redundant feed around any weak interlinks so we can keep *all our weapons* online in a fight." He leaned heavily on his words to make sure she caught his meaning. "While I'm working on it, you might see an over-current error on the instruments."

Cho-shen nodded to confirm his explanation sounded plausible.

"That's what it looks like from here," Santore said. "Thanks for letting me know, by the way."

"We should be half-way to good shortly." He closed the comm from his end.

His comments told her they were starting to feed power from the Creche's reactor in cargo bay three and were almost cobbled together. But only on one of the particle cannon arrays.

She stepped away from the console. "As long as he's working on it, you ought to disable the alarms or we're all going to go insane."

"Are you sure?" the engineer asked, glancing back at the ExO.

She nodded. Firmly. "We've got enough to worry about without an overly sensitive claxon fighting to get attention. Being distracted, and wasting time watching over his shoulder, is low on my list of priorities if the ugly starts." In truth, she didn't want the engineer focusing on the power grid readings and figuring out what they were doing.

If anything went wrong, she didn't want witnesses. That would only bend everything sidewise faster than she could keep it contained.

The Ops officers still had no clue what they were doing in the cargo hold, and she hoped to keep it that way until she was sure about what was really going on with Valleri. For now, there was little she could do other than sit watch and try to contain things if someone got suspicious. It was a critical role but didn't feel like anything other than holding down the deck plating.

What she really wanted was to find evidence supporting her suspicions that Valleri sent the message that stuck the pirates on their tail. Unfortunately, that was proving much more difficult than she expected, since he was the only person on the ship who had any real degree of privacy. It wasn't so much that he was above surveillance, it's just that he had the access codes to control the security system. It made it challenging for her to confirm her suspicions.

At this point all she had was his absence, and a gut feeling. And that wasn't enough.

Sitting in the command seat, with one of the arm mounted control screens open, she had an image of the corridor outside the captain's quarters so she could see if he left and went anywhere in the ship. She also had the optic from the hangar deck on a second window. Neither one had shown any activity since she'd been on watch, but every time she sat down, she scrolled over the records to make sure she hadn't missed anything.

The other arm screen had a view of the comm system, and she was watching for any indication of another signal. The deep-comm transmitter was a massive power drain, so just for good measure, she also kept an eye on the primary power feed through that circuit. She knew it was overkill, but if it was the captain, he'd know more about avoiding detection than anyone on the ship. Probably even her.

"Status report," Valleri said from the door behind her.

Frak! She slapped the toggles to power down both screens just as he stepped into range. She jumped up and spun in his direction. Hopefully, he hadn't seen what she was looking at.

"No changes, Captain," she said, trying to keep her shock from showing on her face. "We're four hours and thirteen minutes from the open threshold drop point at 127 G Centauri. The three raiders behind us are still in formation, over a half light-year astern. They're still spread out equally, thirty degrees off axis."

The helmsman made sure she'd finished then added. "Engines at ninety-two percent. Maintaining speed at 2.5kC."

Valleri nodded, though he didn't turn to face him. He looked like he was about to leave, but instead, glanced at the seat behind her. "Is my chair, da?"

"I didn't expect you on deck for another few hours," she said, not stepping out of his way. The things she's been watching were still open, even though the screens were off. She didn't want to give him any reason to think she was suspicious.

"Is good for you to be rested when we drop to sublight," he said.

She chuckled. "I bleed caffeine. Sleep is for the weak."

He raised an eyebrow and glanced across the deck to the VAT dispenser. "Da, caffeine is good."

Opportunity. "Get your hardball, and then I'll let you have your chair," she said, trying to sound casual.

To log out between the two of them was only a formality. Neither of them worried about transferring command codes for duty shifts, but if she didn't get her butt back in the chair and kill the open files, it was going to be bad.

Of course, if she logged out entirely that would be suspicious too, although that was infinitely better than him catching her spying.

He looked at her strangely for a long second, then headed across the deck. She dropped into the seat, and without opening the screens, entered her command codes into the arm-console to log out. The computer chirped as it accepted the entry, and she bounced back to a standing position before he glanced back at her. He'd probably heard the tones.

Klinestrom tilted his head, and she shot him dead with a glare.

Keep it to yourself.

Fortunately, he nodded and swiveled his seat back toward the helm.

Maybe he was suspicious, too? she wondered. Though it didn't matter, since there was no way she could risk talking to him about it. He was a good officer, and if they made it out of this alive, she'd planned to offer him the post as her ExO.

When Valleri returned with his drink, she stepped to the side and nodded. "The deck is yours, Captain."

"Da. Try to sleep. Will call if trouble starts," he said, dropping into the seat and opening the arm-screen to log in. If he noticed that she'd logged out, he didn't show it.

She realized that she'd been holding her breath as she spun to leave. She let it out slowly and shook her head.

"Sleep is not happening," she muttered as she pushed through the door and out into the corridor. She had a new question to answer before the stink got worse and the darkhats made their move.

How the hell did he get out of his quarters without me seeing?

She knew with more certainty than ever before that the answers to the questions she'd been asking all pointed in the same direction.

Obviously, he'd ghosted the system. But why?

CHAPTER SIXTEEN

To CALL IT ORGANIZED CHAOS would have been polite. It was organized. Vaguely. But it was chaos, through to the bone.

Kylla stood between the two worlds they were trying to manage, simultaneously keeping a foot in each as they pulled in opposite directions.

"Jason says he's never seen anyone work like your people do," Santore said, unexpectedly appearing behind her.

She snapped around to see the ExO watching the activity in the cargo hold. She stared in open disbelief as two men picked up a three-hundred-kilogram emitter guide for one of the particle cannons and shouldered it easily. They disappeared through the hatch into the interconnect.

It was the fourth and final emitter for the second array. That meant they'd finally finished the heavy work. Now it was only the details.

"I see what he meant," she said, shaking her head.

"We usually don't like to show off. It tends to attract inquisitive eyeballs."

"I can see why that might get your eggs in the wind," she said, holding out a cup of coffee.

Kylla looked at it suspiciously.

Santore laughed. "It's real. I stopped by your lab looking for you, and they told me you were here. The doctor said you'd need a dose by now, so he sent it with me."

"Thanks." She took it and smiled. It took an effort to pull her face into anything other than a grimace. "How are they doing in there?"

"He said they had another five hours to go," she said, looking down at the deck.

She leaned against the bulkhead behind her and took a sip of the coffee while she tried to focus on the ExO. "We don't have that do we?"

Santore shook her head. "I don't think so." She pulled out her thinpad and looked at the chrono. "Three hours and thirty-one minutes."

Kylla studied her face as she put it back in her pocket. *She doesn't think we've got that long.* "Something else is coming at us before then?" Kylla asked. "You think it's Valleri, don't you?"

"Why would you say that?" Her eyes flashed a confirmation as clearly as if she'd spoken it out loud.

"You told me you thought something was twisty with him, and that impression's gotten stronger every time we've talked since then."

"Being a plusser also makes you a mind reader?" she asked.

"A face gives away a lot more than people know," she said. "Honestly, at first I thought it was you who was working with the darkhats, but then when you came to ask me what we were doing, I realized that whoever it was, had to be someone who knew already. That left me one choice."

She nodded. But her eyes still said she wasn't convinced that Kylla wasn't a telepath.

"Telepaths are a fluke. We don't know what causes that to manifest in an Augment," she said, trying to put on a reassuring face. "I'm only a technological empath. I do machines, not people. And even then, only ones that are Shan Takhu."

"I have no clue how that would work, but it doesn't matter," Santore said, sweeping a deeper explanation aside for now. "I'm interested in why you'd come to that conclusion."

"Because it's what you believe," she said, shrugging. "I think you've got access to facts I don't have, and those facts point you at him. Since I trust you, I'll accept your conclusion."

Santore raised an eyebrow. "You trust me? Why?"

She stared at her for several seconds. "Because you intentionally let me see what you are thinking."

"Intentionally?"

"I've been upfront about being able to read subconscious signals on a person's face. And you don't pull back. You don't even make an effort to put on a mask."

"Would it help?"

"Probably not," Kylla admitted. "It might make it harder to pick up your micro-expressions if you did, but they'd still be there, just less quick to read."

"That makes it a waste of my effort, and of your time."

"You don't think we've got much of that left to burn," she asked. It wouldn't have been hard for anyone to come to that conclusion, given her expression.

She shook her head. "The captain's been nonexistent on deck for the last two shifts, and suddenly he shows up out of nowhere. Now that he's back I'd wager the shit is about to start stinking."

"You're thinking he sent another message?"

"I don't know." She wobbled her head ambivalently but finally settled on nodding. "It wouldn't do me any good to deny it."

"Why would he have sent the first one?"

"He's got serious short-run syndrome now that he's heading for the day he goes dirtside," she said. "What bothers me is that maybe I saw this coming. He's a career Colonial Wing captain, and he's looking at a minimal pension when he cashiers out."

"As a captain? That's got to be solid comfortable most anywhere he puts down."

Santore snorted and threw in an eye roll for good measure. "You'd be surprised. It's a government job. When you sign on with the Colonial Wing, you put in your sentence and you move up steady. I'll get his seat as soon as he grounds. It's not like FleetCom where you work your ass off and get short stroked to death. Nobody contracts to this Wing because of the income potential, or the retirement plan."

"Did he get a better offer from the pirates?" *From the pirates? The risk of betrayal alone makes that a long way from stacking square.* But she let her question stand.

"A lot of privateers pay for leads. If you know where to look on the Dark Market, it's easy to hook into. Even a two percent finder on what we're carrying would double his lifestyle potential. Not including the extra chit that your fancy polish might add to it."

Kylla wanted to be angry, but she wasn't sure who to be mad at. *When a career of service isn't enough to keep a man honest, is it the man, or the system that left him feeling desperate, that carries the blame?*

In either case, the extra slick tech they were carrying didn't seem enough to be worth it.

"It's all I got for a motive," Santore said. "Unless you know more than I do."

She shook her head, but the feeling that there was something more still lingered. "And he's the only one with opportunity."

"Exactly. There are too many reasons—"

"ExO, report to Operations. Chief Engineer to your station. Code Red. This is not a drill. All hands report to stations. Code

Red." The announcement rang through the sudden silence in the cargo hold.

Santore sprang toward the door, but Kylla caught her arm before she got a full step. "Should I come along?"

"No. He'd just have you removed, and it would make the confusion worse," she said, unclipping her collar comm and handing it to her. "I'll let you know what's going on as soon as I've got anything."

"If it's pirates…"

"The cruise engine is still running, so we didn't hit a mine," she said, with a shrug. "That means, if Valleri didn't hold off on calling the code, we'll have at least a half hour before anyone can get into range. At that point we might need your juice."

"We'll keep working until we can't," she said, letting go of the ExO's elbow and watching her disappear.

Turning back toward her people, she waved her arms. "Break's over. We've got a second gun platform to get operating, and we've got thirty minutes to get it done."

Now the chaos really starts.

CHAPTER SEVENTEEN

"We're about thirty minutes from the Oort safe density threshold," Klinestrom said. "Maybe we can stretch that another five minutes or so, if we have to."

"Maintain course," Valleri said. "Best speed."

Santore had pushed through the hatch and was standing just inside the OpsDeck trying to assess the situation. They were still on cruise, so that was a good sign. "What's our status?"

"Pirates have invited themselves to party," the captain said, without turning to face her. He sat in his seat, looking totally unconcerned. "They were courteous enough to send warning."

"They were?"

"Da," he said, shrugging.

"Where are they?"

"Just under a half light-year aft, closing at 8kC," the sensor officer said. "Twenty-six minutes to weapons range."

"Closing at 8kC? What is our speed?"

"We are maintaining 2k."

"Why did we slow down?"

"We're scanning for mines," Klinestrom said. "But they're driving at almost 10kC."

"What the hell are they?"

"They read like heavy patrol cruisers with modified coils," the sensor officer said. She glanced up, trying to catch the ExO's eye. "At this range it is hard to tell anything other than their adjusted mass and field output."

"Do they know we've picked them up?" she asked.

"Da. Was message from them," Valleri said, turning to glare at her like she was wasting his time for asking so many questions. "We are under orders to stand down and surrender."

"Of course," she said. "Obviously, we haven't done that."

"Not yet. But is no choice," he said. "Is three of them and all are bigger than *Viper*."

"Maybe there's a choice," she said. "Captain may I talk to you a moment."

He shook his head. "I know about guns in cargo hold. Is waste of time."

"Why?" she asked, surprised that he knew, and doubly shocked that he wasn't blowing seals over it.

"If we surrender, we may live. If we fight, is fact we will die."

"These are planetary defense class particle cannon arrays. If we can draw them in and then surprise them—"

"Da. If we use them, we may kill two pirate vessels. We will not get second shot and others will still kill us."

Others? What the frak does he know that we don't?

"Respectfully, sir," she said, lowering her voice and leaning over the back of his chair, "There is no guarantee they won't kill us, anyway. I think we should at least try to defend ourselves, and if we surprise them, maybe they'll back off. Pirates are in it for profit. If we can make the cost too high—"

Twisting, he leaned away so he could look at her. "No. We will make deal to surrender."

"Then why haven't we already dropped to sublight?"

"If we reach edge of system, seventh planet is marginally

habitable. Crew can survive there until rescued. Lifeboat range is limited."

"Then you're planning to abandon ship?"

He shrugged. "Ship and cargo are valuable assets with which to buy safety of crew. Is only concern, da?"

Crew.

"Not the passengers?"

"They are reason we are in stink," he said, clenching his jaw as he bit down on some inner conflict. Turning toward the viewscreen, he waved his hand dismissively. "Decision is made. Notify crew to make ready for boarding parties and to abandon ship. No resistance is to be given."

She stood up stiffly and took a step back, not sure she was believing the order she had just received. *Abandon ship?*

"Is problem?" he asked, without looking at her. He knew her well enough to know she was ready to fight him over it. "Do as I say, or I will remove you from deck."

"Yes, Sir," she said. Her throat felt like she was having to force air through it to get the words out.

He didn't move as she walked over to the comm station.

"He's really going to abandon the *Aggie?*" the comm officer whispered.

"Apparently so," she said. "Open the shipwide comm."

He nodded, keying in the command.

"All hands, this is Executive Officer Ayanna Santore. Under direct command of Captain Grigor Valleri, I am ordering all crew members to stand by for boarding parties." She paused and turned to face the command riser. "The captain further directs the crew to prepare to abandon ship without resistance. I hereby formally add to this announcement that I am issuing this order under protest—"

Valleri launched himself out of his chair and was half-way

across the deck to cut her off when Klinestrom caught him by his arm and spun him back toward his seat. The captain stumbled at the unexpected change in trajectory, but before he had regained his footing, the helmsman had his stunner leveled at the captain. Like all the Ops officers, he'd been issued a sidearm stunner when the Code Red went out. At least two of the others joined him.

Apparently, all they needed to change position was an indication that they weren't alone in disagreeing with the orders.

"Stupid bitch," he roared as Klinestrom nudged him back into his seat with the barrel of his stunner. "They agreed to let us live as long as we hand over passengers."

"When did they do that?" he asked, beating her to the same question. "I didn't hear any such offer." He glanced at Santore before he shrugged.

The ExO slashed her finger across her throat, to cut the shipwide comm. "Captain Valleri, I think you need to be very careful what you say next."

"Is you who need to be careful," he growled, pushing himself back up from the chair and looking around. "Is mutiny?"

"Not yet," she said. "Although I'm willing to make it formal if I need to. It sounds to me like you sold us out."

"They only want passengers and cargo," he said as he took inventory of his position in the rapidly changing social landscape of the OpsDeck. "If we resist, we will die, and they will still take what they want. Is no point in fighting."

Klinestrom turned to face Santore. "The question burning to be asked, is how does he know what they want?"

She nodded. "Care to explain?"

Valleri glared at the helmsman and then turned his attention back to her. "Not to mutineer like you."

Two security handlers appeared at the door with their stunners drawn. Clearly from their expressions, they didn't know who to target. The sensor officer spun and leveled her pistol at them, raising an eyebrow in a way that left no doubt she would drop them both if they made the wrong choice.

Clearing her throat, the ExO stepped up and pulled the captain's collar comm off his coverall. She clipped it around her own neck. "Pursuant to Colonization Command regulations, I am hereby officially relieving Captain Valleri of command, effective immediately, under the grounds of conspiracy to commit criminal acts and recklessly endangering his ship, crew, and payload."

"You will not survive to make charges formal," he growled. "Is you who jeopardize ship."

She ignored his indignation. "Do I have any other command officers that sustain my actions under these grounds?"

Klinestrom stepped forward to stand beside her. "I do."

The engineering officer took a step forward and nodded. So did the sensor officer. She looked at the Comm officer, who was holding a stunner in his hand. He took a deep breath and holstered his weapon but nodded as well. No one else on the Ops crew moved, but none objected either.

"Then take the captain from the OpsDeck and confine him to his quarters. Place a watch on his door and do not let him out under any circumstances. Do I make myself clear?"

"Yes, ma'am," the one standing closest said as he holstered and secured his sidearm. He stepped forward and took Valleri by the elbow. He jerked free of the man's grip but spun and stormed off the deck.

"Lock out the captain's command access codes. ExO authorization, Omega-Epsilon-One-Seven. Enter the change in command into the ship's log and transmit status update to Colonization Command immediately."

"Yes, ma'am," the comm officer said, sitting down to send

the message.

She stepped across the deck and looked down at the captain's seat. Her seat now. But she couldn't bring herself to sit down in it. This wasn't how she wanted to take command of the *Agamemnon*. It wasn't how she ever would have imagined it happening.

"Status update transmitted," the comm officer reported quietly.

She glanced over and nodded. Obviously, this wasn't how any of them expected it to play out. "Open shipwide," she said, turning to face the main screen.

The chirp announced that she was on. "All hands, this is ExO... Acting Captain... Santore. Disregard previous orders. Captain Valleri has been lawfully relieved of duty pending a court of inquiry. As many of you know, we have had three pirate raiders in pursuit for over a day now. They have begun to move into position to attack, and we expect to engage them shortly. Unless we are left with no alternative, we will not be abandoning the *Agamemnon*, or its passengers. Security details prepare to repel enemy combatants. All hands, emergency stations."

She nodded, and the comm cut out. "Now it gets interesting," she whispered.

CHAPTER EIGHTEEN

KYLLA STOOD STARING at the mess that the Incubator Chamber had become. They had unpolarized the window between the Sequencer Lab and the Incubators, and she watched the chaos rolling in waves across the floor. Literally.

It looked unbelievably out of control, although somehow, they were doing the impossible. They'd already transferred the infants and undergrown Augments to medical suspension chambers and were working their way up the age distribution progressively. The medical staff was birthing ten times as many Augments in a single work shift as they normally would have in a month. They'd organized into three teams emerging the newborns from their incubation tubes, and three more working frantically to stabilize their metabolism.

So far none of them had died from the incalculable number of potential complications they faced, but many were still unconscious and there were several more still waiting to emerge.

She watched the process with equal parts fascination and horror, as naked Augments took their first breath of real air, and universally fell into paralyzing fits of explosive coughing. It was almost as psychologically shocking for her to watch the thick mucous-heavy slime erupt from their lungs, as it was for the newborn Augments to experience it.

This wasn't how the process worked.

Ever.

The doctors and med-techs were grinding through the relentless stress on pure brain-numbing adrenaline.

"Holy frak, there's been a mutiny," Dorran said, interrupting her staring as another newly born seventeen-year-old choked his way through his first lungful of air. The fluorocarbon breathing gel exploded out of him, and one of the doctors calmly wiped it off with a pad. He examined it quickly to make sure there was no blood or tissue in it and then tossed the rag to the side and moved on to the next table.

Kylla shook her head and went back to watching the process.

"Did you hear me?" He reached out and touched her before she disengaged from what she was witnessing.

"What?" she glanced up at him.

"Yah," Dorran said. "Santore took Valleri out of the tall seat."

She blinked several times as the reality hammered its way into her brain. "When?"

"Just now. I was on my way back here to see if I could get Solo working to auto target the guns, when the announcements came over the shipwide comm."

"You aren't serious?"

"He is factually correct," Solo said.

"The captain ordered the crew to prepare to abandon ship, and then the comm cut out. A couple minutes later Santore came back on as 'acting captain' and announced that Valleri had been lawfully relieved of command."

"I know she thought he was the one conspiring with the pirates," Kylla said. "I just didn't think it was going to play out—"

The collar comm she'd clipped on her neck chirped. It was Santore's, and she'd forgotten she was wearing it. She tapped the activator. "Yes?"

"I'm sure you've heard that there's a change in the command structure," Santore said.

"Just now," she said, still not sure of the reality. "Congratulations?"

"Yah, this is likely to be the shortest command in history."

"Hopefully not."

"Chief Willis says you people pulled off a Miracle Mike and got both arrays set up, but we haven't tested targeting control yet."

She glanced over at the engineer. "Dorran and Solo are working on it right now."

"They need to expedite it. We've got problems right on top of us."

She nodded, pointing at the situational display they'd already set up. Dorran jumped toward it.

"Do you have your operations finished?" Santore asked.

"Unloading the Incubators? Not yet. We've got another dozen or so to go. We're getting close."

"We'll stay at cruise as long as we can, but you need to understand that once we drop out, they'll be on us almost instantly. We're watching the density of the 127 G Centauri Oort debris field, and when it exceeds our safety limit, we have to shut down. Best guess is that you've got under twenty minutes until we have to transfer power from your reactor to the arrays."

"We'll need access to external sensors as soon as you can give it to us," Dorran hollered from across the lab. He was at the holographic display and frantically setting up a control interface.

"We're working on it," Willis said, cutting in on the comm. "Three minutes."

"Did you get that?" Kylla asked, glancing over to see him nod. "I'll also pass the word to the medics and see what they can do.

I think they're running long of twenty minutes."

"Understood, but if we don't have the ability to shunt power and hold them off, this is going to turn into a bar brawl."

"I'll get my people deployed into position to back your handlers up, just in case it goes ugly side up."

"I don't think there is a side of this that isn't shit-muckle brown," Santore said, cutting the comm from her end.

Kylla closed her eyes for a second and tried to shut out the chaos long enough to think.

One of the body-mod Augments stood just inside the door. He carried one of their encrypted command comms on his belt. Because they worked on a different protocol and band than the ship's comm, it gave them secure communications even while they were aboard. It wasn't that she had anything to hide, she just knew she needed not to jam up official channels with their own chatter.

They had a limited number of the command comm sets and they'd only deployed them to their fire teams in the last half hour. She waved for him to come over to the table as she collapsed into a seat. He held out his headset to her, and she clipped it over her ear. "This is Kylla Torrance. All Guardian units report to positions and prepare to assist *Agamemnon* security personnel in repelling boarding parties. All non-physical Augments take up positions as possible in, and around, lifeboat access corridors. Do not interfere with the ship's crew under any circumstances but stand by in case we need to abandon ship. Updates will follow as they are available."

"Guardians?" Dorran asked. He didn't look up, but she could tell he approved of the name she'd given to the ones who were about to be amateur soldiers.

"Why not?"

"Give them a name to be proud of," he said as the screen in

front of him lit up and he nodded. "If we get the doors open and the racks extended, at least we'll be able to kick some pirate ass."

Pushing herself up from the table, she suddenly felt most of her real age. It crashed down on her shoulders like a bag of boulders as she shuffled over to the intercom into the Incubator Chamber and punched the toggle. "You've got ten minutes before we might need to steal the lights. Can you do it?"

"Frak no," Adam said. She watched him stand up straight and look down the row of incubator tubes still containing bodies. "We've got seven to emerge... and twelve to renormalize their metabolism. I need another hour."

"If you're lucky, you've got fifteen minutes. Probably less."

He dropped his head forward and looked like he was going to follow his forehead to the floor. "We're almost ready to start into the T-r Series run. They're the first run of broad range Augments we've ever sequenced. That makes them the most complex to normalize. We might get them all breathing air in fifteen, if we drop everything else, but without power there is no way we'll be able to slow them down. They'll be lucky to last a few days without that, if things go sidewise."

"What happens if you don't get them out before we have to divert power?"

"They'll be dead in minutes," Dr. Wang said. She looked like she was covered in globs of fluorocarbon gel as she stepped around the end of a medical table.

Adam turned and faced the window as he flipped his surgical visor up to make sure she could see his face clearly. He obviously wanted her to understand he was serious. "It would be more merciful not to pull them, if we can't get them stabilized."

"Just get them out," Kylla said. "We'll figure out how to keep them alive later. If any of us make it that far."

CHAPTER NINETEEN

"WE'RE GETTING CLOSE to the threshold," Klinestrom said. "Another minute or less before we pass the safety line at this velocity."

"If we reduce speed, can we push deeper?"

He shook his head. "As big as we are, we don't have the maneuverability to risk it. I already passed the redline but the debris density is climbing fast."

All it took was a miniscule space rock with enough mass to push through their field to end them. A superluminal impact with a grain of sand released enough energy to blow them clear out of space. They wouldn't even know they were dead before the ship and everything for ten-thousand klick incinerated with them.

The farther they pushed into the star's Oort cloud, the more likely that eventuality became.

"How long will we have once we drop?"

"Three minutes, depending on how deep they push," Hansen said. They were running all three shifts on deck to cover the stations in case they had to fight. Three sensor officers stood at the console.

"They have a smaller draft," Klinestrom said. "They won't

hesitate to dive this deep."

She nodded toward the comm officer and waited for the chirp that told her she was live. "All hands prepare to secure from cruise. Security teams to stations. We will be engaging enemy forces within five minutes." She slashed her finger across her throat to cut the shipwide.

"Engineering, are we ready with our little surprise?"

"Aye, Boss," Willis said. "As soon as they shunt the power to us, we're good to eat us a couple pirate ships."

"Who's got the targeting control?"

"We do," a voice she recognized as the lead engineer for the plussers answered. "We're standing by for you to pick your target, Captain."

Her title still rang strangely in her ears, but she knew she didn't have time to worry over it, so she buried her reaction. "Are you ready with your other project?"

"Not yet. Another few minutes if you can give it to us," Kylla said.

"If they come straight in on us, you might have three," she said.

She sighed. "Understood. I'll pass the word." She sounded like she had boulders raining down on her.

"Open the bay doors and prepare to extend the arrays," Santore said.

"Mr. Klinestrom drop us to sublight," she said. "Sensors, I want active scanning as soon as the photon boom clears."

"Yes, ma'am," she said, as the *Agamemnon*'s cruise engine shut down.

A rainbow cascade of light washed over the forward viewscreen and out into normal space as the trapped photons leapt free of the collapsing field.

"Engineering let's get those racks out there and get the

cannons precharged," she said before the kaleidoscopic light show had completely dissipated. "There's no use in hiding that we intend to fight. Maybe we can keep them outside their own firing range once they see what we're swinging."

The particle cannons could easily punch upward from the surface of a planet to take out a ship in orbit. Without the atmosphere to disrupt the first couple hundred klick of the beam, they'd be good for double the range of any standard space-based beam weapon.

"Arm the repelling lasers and sync targeting control to the AA for anti-missile defense."

"Yes, ma'am," the second helmsman said as he entered the commands.

"Do we have a heading?" Klinestrom asked.

She sat down on the edge of the command chair as she sorted their options.

If they went deeper toward the inner system, they'd be in a denser region of the Oort field, which meant they'd lose maneuverability with respect to the far more nimble pirate raiders. But if they sat still, they'd be a simple target for a missile volley.

Neither option was much to consider.

Finally, she shrugged. "No heading. Maintain station keeping but bring us around to face them square. Let's line up so that if they drop close, we can get a first shot before they realize what we're packing."

One thing she knew was that pirates liked to make a dramatic entrance and jumping in close was always a way to swing your eggs. Depending on how accurately they could track the raiders as they came in, maybe they could scramble some of them before it got uglier.

"What have we got on sensors?"

"Stand by," Hansen said. "The three ships behind us have slowed down."

"What?" she asked, jumping across the deck to confirm what he'd said.

He nodded, stepping to the side to make room for her. "But we've got another problem. There are three new targets approaching from down-system."

Frak! *Valleri knew there were more ships. Damn him*! "Where are they?"

"Bearing zero-zero seven by three-ten. Range 800 kiloklick and closing."

"Can you tell what they are?" She stepped back and turned toward the helm.

"One looks like a light raider. Small. Maybe the same class as the *Viper*. The other one is a large commercial freighter or passenger ship. It's throwing a long field, so it might be pulling a train of containers."

"You said there were three," Santore said.

"There are. But the other one, I don't know what the hell it is," he said, looking up and shrugging. "It's got a power signature that I've never seen before."

"What does that mean?"

"This thing is radiating almost nothing electrodynamic, but it has a mass field that's at least double ours."

"How big is it?"

"Extremely small," she said. "The inertial field spread is under seventy-five meters post to post, but it's dense. In the teraCochrane range."

"Are you sure you're reading that right?" Santore asked.

The *Agamemnon*'s coils were only two megaCochrane, and they created a stable cruise field almost two thousand meters across.

She nodded and put her data up as an overlay on the main screen. The two normal ships were clearly visible as ripples on the G/I sensors, but the third one looked almost like a pinhole in the surrounding space.

"How's that possible?" Klinestrom asked, glancing over his shoulder at Santore.

She shook her head. "A field that dense would take a singularity to produce."

"You don't think—"

"We're being hailed," the comm officer interrupted. "Audio only."

"*Agamemnon*, stand down immediately." A female voice said. From her tone, she expected her words to be taken as an order.

"Who is this?" Santore said.

"Where is Valleri?"

"He's been removed from command," she said, taking a deep breath and trying to keep the woman's condescension from baiting her into something premature. "I want to know who you are."

"That's unfortunate. Is he alive?" she asked, ignoring Santore's question for the second time.

"That's not your concern," she said. "I'm the captain, and that makes me the one you need to talk to. Identify yourself or we're done here."

"He was a smart man. Are you smart enough to take the deal we offered him?"

"I'm smart enough to know not to make a deal with someone who won't identify themselves."

The main viewscreen flickered and a woman's face appeared. She looked younger than she sounded, with smooth dark skin and flashing eyes that sparked icy blue and white. "I am Nandia N'gabo. Captain of the *Seeker*."

Santore stood up. "I'm—"

"Ayanna Santore. Yes, I know who you are," she said dismissively. "Now can we get back to business? I asked if you were smart enough to complete the deal we offered Valleri?"

"And what deal was that?"

"Obviously, he didn't trust you with his plans," she said, rolling her eyes. "What I offered was safe passage to anywhere you want to retire, with enough chit to make sure you never remember what happened here today. I only want some of your passengers."

"The passengers?"

"Yes. Very few of them, in fact. The one with the third eye and all her type."

"That's a strange request for a pirate. Looking for slaves?"

She laughed. "I am most assuredly not a pirate, although I do work with them when I need to. But that's one of the things you need to forget."

There has to be an angle here. I just have to keep digging, she thought. "If you only want the passengers, what happens to the ship?"

"My associates get the ship, and the cargo, and you and your officers retire to someplace like Escabosa, and drink fruity alcohol for the rest of your lives."

"Two of her ships are almost on top of us," the sensor tech said over her earpiece. "The strange one stopped at 500 kiloklick."

"And if I decline your offer?"

N'gabo laughed again, but this time it was a chilling sound. "Resistance is irrelevant. If you try, we'll still take the passengers we want, and the ships behind you will take the *Agamemnon*, anyway. If you choose to play that way, the only difference is that there will be a lot more blood spilled."

"You seem awfully sure of yourself," Santore said.

"It's your call, Captain. You have ten seconds to decide, and then I withdraw my offer."

"You're bluffing."

The screen went dark, but not before she shot Santore a strangely bemused look.

"Are the two other ships in range?" she asked as soon as she was sure the comm had dropped entirely.

The sensor officer nodded. "Barely."

"Let's see if we can spill first blood and maybe make her think about it," she said. "Target both ships and fire."

There was a bright flash of light to starboard as the particle cannons opened up the hull of the larger carrier ship.

Then absolute darkness swallowed everything as a hammer blow drove anything not firmly anchored in place across the deck. It felt like the gravity plating had rotated ninety degrees for an instant... before it shut off entirely.

Along with everything else.

CHAPTER TWENTY

"What the frak just happened? It feels like we hit something."
Dorran's voice echoed out of the sudden silence. It was only a
few seconds after the universe had tumbled sidewise, but once
the clatter of crashing… everything… ended, the silence was
profound.

Kylla knew instantly what it was, and her heart froze solid
in her chest.

"It's a Hound," she whispered as she pulled herself out from
under the console where the impact had tossed her. They were
weightless, but she knew that might be temporary, so she tried to
orient herself upright with respect to the floor, in case downward
chose to reassert itself unexpectedly. It was extra difficult with
the total absence of light.

"A hound?" he asked. He groaned but sounded like he was
pulling himself into a chair.

"It's an old Earth phrase for a slave hunter."

"I didn't know that was a real thing," he said. "Why do you
say that's what it is?"

"I'd wager my last chit that was a quantum gravity pulse,"
she said.

A strange belching sound echoed out of the dark. "Given

the evidence available, I would say that is a valid assessment," Solo croaked as its vocal processor reorganized its subroutines. "I also concur that there is a high probability that it is an Institute sanctioned Hound."

"Why aren't you down?" the engineer asked.

"I am equipped with a local power module and utilize distributed architecture code. I have completed restoration from my backup files."

"Already?"

"Distributed Awareness code was originally designed to take over any hostile quantum-hybrid awareness in milliseconds. To take over my own processor array is on the same order of difficulty."

"That's a useful ability," Dorran said. "A bit unsettling, but I'm glad you're a good guy."

"I am neither good nor evil, I am simply—"

"What's the status in the ship?" Kylla asked, cutting off what could become a long discussion. They were in trouble and didn't have time for it.

"The main AA will be offline for several hours while it reloads, although I can access portions of its internal network directly if needed. Damage control parties are currently initializing the *Agamemnon*'s emergency response systems. Gravity plating is restoring throughout most of the ship itself, however the passenger wards and cargo holds are still without gravity or power. Primary shipwide life support is offline. Main reactors are offline. Our external sensor tie-in is offline."

"Did we get either of the two ships we were targeting?" he asked.

"Before our link went down, I could confirm that the larger ship was critically damaged. Unfortunately, the other target did not appear to be impacted."

"Is it possible that it was a shockwave from the enemy target coming apart?" Dorran asked. He'd settled into position near the table.

"Doubtful, the thrust vector does not line up with the bearing of the ship we hit."

"What about our systems?" Kylla asked.

"Our power will be reset momentarily. The secondary antimatter injectors were in standby mode and have engaged. Once the flow containment interlinks reestablish, we will have full power. We do currently have backup life support."

"Warn the Incubator Chamber before you give them a floor," Dorran said.

"I have not already established gravity plating because I have no comm to the Incubator work area," Solo said. "There may be damage from fluorocarbon contamination of the circuitry."

"Frak," she hissed, bracing to launch herself toward the Chamber door.

"I'm on it," the body-mod who'd been in the room said. She couldn't see where he was in the lab other than to tell he was in motion. She could hear the air moving as he flew several meters above the floor at a dangerous velocity.

"Wait, I'll take care of that," she said, triangulating on his turbulence and reaching out to snag his leg as he blew past her. She'd anchored herself to the console with her opposite arm and managed to stop his inertia in spite of the fact that he was easily double her mass. Pulling him back toward where she knew the chair had been, she explained what she wanted him to do. "If your command comm is still working, I want you to pass the word that we need manpower to evacuate the Creche. Have your people position themselves to provide cover and then have anyone not directly involved here start boarding the lifeboats."

"I wouldn't wager they can launch the boats if the power's

down," Dorran said.

"I'm sure there's a manual launch system," she said. "It would be stupid to plan an emergency evacuation system without a backup."

Hopefully.

"Naval architects aren't—"

She waved her hand as the lights came back up and she blinked repeatedly to ratchet them down against sudden brightness. "It doesn't matter. If we've got a Hound on us, we've got to scatter if we can. Just get them moving," she ordered, despite knowing that the odds of any of them escaping were skinny.

Their guard pushed off the console toward the main entrance to the lab with a grunt. Lowering his voice, he started passing out marching orders.

"We are ready to restore full power and gravity," Solo said.

"Dorran, I want you to go let them know in the Incubator Chamber that we're about to restore the floor, and that we've got bodies on the way to help them evacuate," she said, making a decision as the seed of an idea coalesced in her brain. "If Adam pushes back, don't waste time arguing. Do what you have to in order to get compliance. Is that clear?"

"Not really," he said, shaking his head and refusing to move. "What are you planning? I might have had a tube for a momma, but I know what it means when the parents send the kids away."

"Just do what I say," she said. "Solo and I are going to buy time if we can."

"How?"

"I have to surrender," she admitted. "Alright?"

"Not today," Solo said.

"I don't have time for your misguided nobility. Either of you. I have an idea and I don't really intend to surrender, but if you don't both do your part, it won't work. Just do what I say."

Dorran started to protest again, but she cut him off with a glare.

"If that was a focused quantum gravity pulse, that means whatever ship sent it is at least reinforced with Shan Takhu Tech."

"That is a valid assumption," the AA said.

"Apparently neither of you remember that I'm one of the few people aboard the *Agamemnon* that has the ability and experience to access that technology?" she said. "If I can get aboard that ship, without being dead first, I might be able to do more than just buy time."

"That's a long odds—"

Santore's collarcomm chirped around her neck and she jabbed a finger toward the door to the Incubator Chamber. "MOVE!"

"Santore to Kylla Torrance. What's your status?"

"We're alive, and we've got power and life support. We're checking on the Incubators now."

"The *Aggie*'s dead in the water, and we've got a problem up here," Santore said. "I think they're looking for you. Specifically."

"I expected as much. I need to take care of a few things and then I'm ready to give myself up. Hopefully, you can use my surrender to negotiate your way out of this."

"Negotiate? How do we do that? We haven't even gotten the comm operating."

"I need to get a team together and we're on our way. Just stall for a couple minutes."

"The only stalling is going to be done at gunpoint. After they come aboard," she said, growling in frustration. "So far, they haven't launched any boarding parties, but they might be waiting for the real pirates to soften us up."

"Real pirates? Then you know it's not pirates who hit us," Kylla asked.

"That's what she says, but I didn't check her identity records."

"She?" Kylla closed her eyes and pounded her fist against her forehead. "Did she tell you her name was N'gabo?"

"You know her?"

"Worse. I know who made her," she said.

CHAPTER TWENTY-ONE

By the time they got to the OpsDeck, the raiding parties had started. The floor shook as Kylla stepped through the door. Dorran, and three of the newborn T-r Series Augments were with her.

She'd had to lie to Adam to get him to let her take any of them. She knew she'd betrayed his trust, but she had no choice. If any of the new Augments were going to survive, the five of them had to take the risk.

Stopping just inside, she pointed to the side and made it clear she wanted them to stay back.

"Breaching charge! Deck seven, crew quarters," the engineering officer bellowed. She sounded terrified.

"Security handlers are responding," the comm officer said, much more calmly.

Another rumble rattled the plates, and the lights flickered in the overhead.

"Primary power, deck two. We're back on batteries," the engineer said. Clearing her throat, she tried to sound less like she was sucking helium as she went on, "Damage control teams report to junction—"

"Wait, you need to tell them to disengage and abandon ship,"

Kylla yelled, raising her voice to cut through the chaos.

"What?" Santore spun and glared at her. "Is that how you intend to negotiate? To give up?"

She nodded. "There's no hand where you're going to save the *Aggie*. Save lives and make the call."

She shook her head. "Fuck you. If that's all you've got, get off my deck."

Kylla stumbled towards her as another explosion caused the gravity plating to surge in ripples. "Ayanna, please listen to me." She grabbed Santore by the arm and dragged her off to the side and out of earshot of the other officers. "Give me one minute to explain."

"I don't have one minute," she said.

"You do, and I do have a plan, but I can't explain it to you," she said. "N'gabo is a Contact Telepath."

"What's the plan?" she growled.

"We're going to take over her ship, and I need your skills as a shipmaster when we do it."

"Take over her ship? The way it's swinging now, I don't even think I can get off this deck alive, let alone over… to her… ship…" Her voice faltered as her mind suddenly played back what Kayla had said far enough that her mouth ran out of fuel. "You said she's a telepath? Then why the frak did you tell me this?"

"Yah, you're not going to like this part." Pulling a stunner out of the back of her coverall, Kylla squeezed off two quick rounds. She could still feel the electrical pulses of the neuro-pellets discharging as she grabbed the front of Santore's uniform and eased her toward the floor. "Frakking ouch!" she hissed. "Sorry Captain, but at least now you can't give away our secret."

Hearing the hissing crackle of the stunner, Klinestrom spun and started to leap toward where Santore had crumpled, but one of the new Augments shot across the deck and shoved him back into his seat. She moved so fast that it was almost impossible to recognize what had happened.

He was moving. Then he was sitting again. Somewhere in that, there was a whooshing of air, and crashing of butt against seat.

It sounded painful.

Damn she's quick. Smart too, Kylla thought, as she shook off the tingle from the stunner and stepped over to kneel in front of Klinestrom. She still held the pistol in her hand and aimed it between his knees. From his expression she could tell he didn't want the intended shot to land where she had it targeted, even accidentally. "You're in charge for now," she said, smiling innocently while she fluttered her optic with the tip of her tongue.

He glanced up for only an instant as the impending danger to his eggs clearly held priority.

"I need you to order everyone else off the OpsDeck," she said, tapping the end of the stunner against his inner thigh. "Tell them its time to abandon ship."

"Everybody stand down," he squeaked. "Get to the escape pods."

"Excuse me?" the comm officer asked.

He jerked his head up and down nervously. "Just do it. Go. I don't know what's going on here, but I think it's time to say goodnight."

"But—"

"Maybe you didn't hear what Mr. Klinestrom said," Kylla said, enunciating her words clearly. She stood up and pointed toward the door with her unoccupied hand. "Get to the escape pods while you can. You're abandoning ship."

One of the other T-r Series Augments leapt over in a single

stride and picked up the sensor tech. He resisted, but it made no difference as he carried him to the door and tossed him through it.

The two security handlers who had been outside in the corridor, heard him screaming and charged onto the OpsDeck with their pistols drawn. The third Augment stood to the side of the door and as they entered casually swatted their weapons away. His enhanced strength translated to speed, and before they skidded to a halt, he'd snatched the handlers off the floor and hurled them ten meters out into the hall.

The comm and sensor officers tapped out, jumping up to run without further coercion.

"Seal and bar the door," she said quietly. "We won't be leaving that way, and we don't want the real pirates interrupting us."

"So, she really isn't a pirate?" Klinestrom asked, still staring at the stunner, even though it was a lot less intimately aimed. "What the hell's going on here?"

"Honestly, the less you know the better," she said, shrugging. Reaching into her pocket, she pulled out one of their command comm transmitters and held it out to him. "When I tell you to, I want you to use that to tell N'gabo we tried to take over Ops, but that you captured us. Make sure she understands you have me in particular, and that you're holding us on the OpsDeck. Be sure you tell her you want to make a deal for passage."

"That's what she offered Valleri and Santore," he said.

"I suspected as much," she said. "It's right out of the manual."

"Hounds have a manual?" Dorran asked from across the deck. He and the third Augment were bending the hatch locking pins so they wouldn't open. Probably ever. It sounded like the breaching charges were over. It was eerily quiet, other than the creaking of the metal twisting as they sealed the door.

She ignored the sarcasm and kept her attention on Klinestrom.

"It's really important that you sell her on the idea that you're serious. She has to believe you, or this isn't going to work. Do you understand me?"

He shook his head before he changed his mind and nodded. "I'll try."

"There is no try," she said, turning and walking over to the three new Augments.

They were all only wearing thinskins and looking like they'd just come from an intense physical workout. It was probably because they were still running at twenty times the normal metabolic rate and burning calories at an impossible rate.

The female showed the least sign of her screaming metabolism, so she handed her the captain's stunner. "Augments always name themselves based on their run series identifier. Have you picked a name for yourself, little one?"

"I was thinking Tia. And maybe Rayce."

She shrugged. "I like it. Here's what I want you to do, Tia," she said, lowering her voice to a dead whisper and leaning in. "As soon as Mr. Klinestrom finishes his message to N'gabo, you need to use that and put him down. Under no circumstances is he to be awake when N'gabo comes through the door."

Tia nodded, shifting the stunner pistol in in her hand and glancing back at the mangled latch on the door.

"She'll use a Shan Takhu jump door and might appear anywhere on the deck. Offer no resistance to anything she does or says. Your only objective is to make sure they take all of us with them back to her ship. That shouldn't be a problem since she won't want to leave witnesses." Kylla tilted her head toward Santore. "Don't even let her leave them."

"You said N'gabo was a telepath?"

"Exactly. She's an extremely adept Contact Telepath. She needs to connect physically to a person to read a mind, but since you three are not normalized, I'm wagering that your synaptic pathways are running too fast for her to sync with. I hope that means she won't be able to read your minds."

"What about me?" Dorran interrupted. He stood off to the side a bit, watching the helmsman fiddle with the command comm. "I'm just running at normal speed."

"I need you awake to be the voice of experience," she said, glancing over at him. "The less you know about the specifics, the better."

"I already know you have a plan," he said.

"It won't matter if she thinks I have a plan," she said. "She needs to take us into custody enough that she'll risk it. As long as I'm unconscious, she'll assume she has control of the situation."

He hauled in a deep breath to protest, but before he could form a word, she cut him off with a wave of her finger.

"Just don't fight her when she gets here. Because she can't read their thoughts, I'm hoping she'll give up and read you."

"And I'm just supposed to stand around and be a pretty picture?" He glared at her.

"You're pretty good at that part," she said with a wink and a quick scan down his anatomy. "But you'll know what to do if it goes sidewise."

She could tell he wanted to keep arguing, but bit back on it and nodded.

Turning away from him, she reached into her coverall and pulled out a thinpad. Tapping an authorization code into the screen, she waited as a file unspooled. "*Acknowledged. Standing by*," flashed on the screen briefly before a second message appeared. "*Good luck*."

The screen went dark as Solo forced the unit into low-power mode.

It's all in your hands now, my friend.

129

She slipped the thinpad back under her clothes, pushing it deep under her thinskin to make sure it wasn't easily found if one of N'gabo's handlers got overly friendly. She had no clue how well disciplined her crew was, and the pheromone fog tended to make everyone a little grabby.

"Alright, Mr. Klinestrom, it's your turn," she said. "Make the call."

He cleared his throat nervously and powered up the command comm.

Turning back to face Tia, she whispered, "You know what to do when he's done."

The Augment nodded.

"Shoot me." She let out a quick huff of air and closed her eyes. "This is going to hurt."

She was right. It hurt a lot.

CHAPTER TWENTY-TWO

FOUR, OVERLY MUSCLED, and heavily armed, soldiers stepped out of thin air near the main viewscreen, and onto the front of the OpsDeck. It looked like they'd walked through the screen and it would have been impossible to tell where they'd come from if Dorran hadn't seen the slight distortion in the light just before they appeared.

Kylla had told him about the Shan Takhu jump doors, but like almost everyone else in the Coalition, he'd never seen one used, and it was disconcerting to see someone appear without warning.

They all wore dark body armor with helmets and optical sensors mounted to thin packs on their backs. It looked like some sort of EVA suit, except for the plating. They were tooled as an assault team.

"Where's Klinestrom?" the tallest of the men growled as he skirted sidewise around the side of the room. The other men fanned out until they'd taken flanking positions on opposite sides of the deck.

Dorran pointed at the unconscious man crumpled beside the helm console, but he kept his attention on the one asking the questions. He was obviously in charge of the team. A single seven-pointed star glinted on his collar. As he got closer, he picked out the man's name from his helmet. *Anders.*

"What happened to him?" Anders asked.

"She stunned him when we found out he was selling us out," he said, tilting his head toward Tia. She held a stunner pistol pinched loosely by the bottom end of the handgrip.

One of the other guards lunged forward and snatched it out of her hand.

"Why didn't you run?" he asked, coming up and staring at Dorran like he was sizing up a slab of cloned protein in an underground market.

Dorran looked toward the door and raised an eyebrow. The mangled locking pins were obvious. "We're trapped between you and, well, a steel bulkhead."

"You're the fugitive plussers Klinestrom was talking about?"

"I didn't know we were fugitives, but you're obviously cognitively under-developed, even for a Cro-Magnon," he said, drawing a swift crack of a gun stock across his face. It split the skin but didn't twist his head sidewise.

"If we're hunting you, then you're runners," Anders said, squinting as it soaked in that he hadn't knocked Dorran back as much as a single step. "You're a body-mod?"

"I'm an engineer," he said, wiping the blood from his cheek with the back of his hand. "Obviously, you aren't N'gabo. I assume she'd have to be smarter than you. Cuter too."

"Who the fuck are you?" Anders growled, clearly contemplating taking a second swing.

"Engineer-Three, Dorran James, at your service."

"Where's Torrance?" he asked, glancing around.

He nodded at one of the two unconscious women on the deck. "And before you ask, that one over there is Ayanna Santore. I guess she's the captain."

Anders stepped over and nudged Kylla onto her back to look at her face. Her optic poked out of her cheek and he smiled. "Yah, that's her."

He tapped into an earpiece commset. "Confirmed, we've got the primary." He paused and listened to instructions. "Yes, ma'am. Beginning containment."

Containment? Dorran's heart nearly skipped a beat. The situation felt like it was going sidewise at light-speed. "Is that a euphemism for taking care of witnesses?"

"What about Valleri?" One of the others asked before he could answer. His helmet identified him as York.

The engineer shrugged. "Last I heard, Santore chained him in his quarters."

"Where are his quarters?" York asked.

"They kept us down in the passenger wards. I think someone said he lived on deck three?"

York shook his head. "Freelancers reported a hard vacuum on three. Somebody dumped the air with a breaching charge before they sealed."

"More balls than brains," Anders said, shaking his head in frustration.

"Then I'm glad the door's sealed." Dorran shrugged. "She was Acting Captain, but if Valleri's sucked a lungful of space, I guess that makes her promotion permanent."

"What happened to her?" Anders asked, looking down at Santore.

"It was a bit of a frakwad, and I'm not really sure who shot first," he said. "They should all be waking up in a while, so you can ask them. I was hiding behind that chair over there, and I didn't see for sure who did what." He pointed his chin toward the captain's seat.

"This reeks like a burnt biscuit," the third one said.

"Nojo, Carmichael," Anders snorted. "Commander Obvious strikes again. I'm not buying it."

"Then I'm glad I'm not trying to sell it. I never was good at sales," Dorran said, turning his head and tapping the other side of his face with a finger. Anders pulled his gun back but stopped before he landed the blow. "You're a sick one, aren't you?"

"I've been called worse by prettier boys than you," he said with a wink. This time the blow landed, but he rolled back to absorb the impact without another cut.

"What are we supposed to do?" York asked.

"Watch them. I'll run it uphill and see where she wants to bury them," he said, stepping across the deck and tapping his earpiece again. Keeping his rifle leveled at Dorran, he covered his mouth as he explained the situation.

"He's telling his boss that he thinks it's a trap," Tia whispered. "He wants to shoot us and—"

"Shut up," Carmichael said, raising his pistol and setting the barrel against the middle of her forehead. It was only a stunner, but at zero-range it could still shatter a skull.

"Easy, we're not giving you any pushback," Dorran said, shooting her a warning glare. *Don't antagonize them.*

"Nobody'd notice one less runaway," he said, clicking the lockout off and slipping his finger against the trigger stud.

"She's just newborn," he pleaded, holding his hands up. "Give her a break, alright?"

"You said she's a newborn?" Anders asked from where he stood.

That got his attention. Dorran tried not to let on that he recognized an opportunity. *How the hell do I work it?*

"How old is she?"

He shrugged. "An hour? Two maybe."

"You've got a Creche on the *Agamemnon*?" Anders walked

back over and nudged Carmichael out of the way with an elbow. He stepped in close and tilted his head to the side as he studied her.

"I asked you a question," Anders said, raising his rifle and pointing it at Dorran's stomach without looking away from her. He thumbed the setting toggle from stun to lethal. "Do you have a Creche with you?"

The engineer stared at the floor but didn't answer.

Spinning the rifle like a club, he swung it toward Tia. It wiffed through empty air where she had been standing. She'd only leaned far enough to the side to give him a clean miss, but the speed she moved left no doubt she was a top tier Augment.

The other three men jumped back and snapped their weapons into position.

"Frak!" Carmichael hissed. It didn't take a mind reader to know he'd just figured out he'd been standing way too close to an apex predator for his own health.

"Well that changes things a little," Anders said as he laughed. Easing himself carefully out of reach, he tapped the stud on his earpiece. "Yes, ma'am she's definitely an Augment," he said. "Honestly, she smells newly punched out too. Strongest phcromones I've ever run into."

After a brief pause while he listened to instructions, he slipped a hand into a pouch on his belt and pulled out several sets of cinch strips. Without looking away, he held them out. "Carmichael, bind them all."

He glanced at the three unconscious bodies on the floor. "Eddington, do them while we're at it. Her Ladyship wants no surprises when she meets them."

"She's coming here?" Dorran asked as Carmichael yanked his arms behind his back and zipped the binder around his wrists.

"She's not much for pirate parties," Anders said, shaking his head and rolling his eyes. "Idiots like things that go boom too much for her taste."

"See, I knew she had to be smarter than you," he said. "So, what comes next?"

"You ask a lot of questions for a prisoner." Carmichael zipped a second and third loop into place. He pulled them tighter, and they bit in painfully. "Bagged and tagged," he added, thumping Dorran on the back of the head to shove him forward.

Anders grabbed him by the shoulder and dragged him off balance. Marching across the deck, he jammed the engineer against a bulkhead near where they'd all appeared and shoved the muzzle of his rifle against the back of his skull. "You're all going for a long walk," he snarled.

The realization that all it took was a twitch of Anders' finger to send this into the deep dark, was enough to keep Dorran pinned effectively in place. And his mouth firmly shut.

I'd wager this isn't remotely similar to anything in Kylla's plan.

CHAPTER TWENTY-THREE

JASON WILLIS WATCHED helplessly as, section by section, the internal sensor grid went offline.

By design, the *Agamemnon*'s engineering section was a self-sufficient fortress, with its own fusion reactor and life support. After the initial shock wave crippled everything, they'd locked down and done manual resets on all their independent systems. Even if it was inevitable, Main Engineering would be the last place on the ship to fall.

Because they had light and air, it was also where their handlers fell back when they needed to regroup, tend to their wounded, or get air in their lungs. Those who were still able to fight, went back out, and those who couldn't, helped him fill in the gaps in his sensors with firsthand reports of what was happening as the pirates pushed deeper into the ship.

Unfortunately, as the situation got worse, there were fewer of their security handlers to take up the battle, and even fewer bringing him the information he needed to make decisions.

"Deck three's a hard vacuum," one handler reported as a medic sprayed dermacast over his broken arm. He was sitting on the edge of a workbench they'd cleared off for triage. "Everybody above there's either dead or cut off."

Willis pulled up a status screen on his portable control pad and scrolled through the data until he found the pod logs. He bit down on his lip and shook his head.

Of the hundred escape pods that served those decks, only a dozen or so showed as jettisoned. Either the boarding parties had captured almost everyone, or there was no one alive to fire them off.

Deck three was also where most of the crew quarters were. Hopefully, that meant everyone had been on duty when it happened.

"What's the status below there?" he asked.

"Six through twelve are continuous running firefights," the handler said. "We're trying to keep your escape routes to the lifeboats open as long as possible. Biggest problem is that it's getting hard to breathe."

He nodded. "Life support's down everywhere but here."

The medic looked over at him. "Low O2 levels in the air means they're suffering from deprivation fugue. It'll be worse the more they exert."

The handler nodded. "The pirate fighters are wearing body armor with their own portable air supplies. They just won't fall over."

Willis looked down at the deck and shook his head. It's just a matter of time. *Eventually they'll win by attrition.*

"How many have we got left?" he asked.

"Under twenty handlers, plus your engine crew," he said. "And a buttload of screaming crazy passengers."

"You mean they haven't jumped ship yet?" Willis asked.

He shook his head. "One of them told me they were waiting for you to make the call."

"Me?"

"Yah, they say you're big-man-in-the-chair at this point," he said. "They know Ops went flatline when the upper sections vented. That makes it your bag of beans."

"How do they know that? I don't even have a live optic link to the OpsDeck."

"A lot of them are carrying sidearms and portable commsets," he said. "They had somebody up there with a comm when the emergency bulkheads gated closed."

"That's more than I know," Willis said, shaking his head.

The handler shrugged with his one good shoulder. "All I know is they're waiting for you to punch us out."

Frak it all to fucking hell. This is not in my job description.

Willis drummed his fist against his forehead while he chewed over what he knew he had to do. It wasn't even a matter of choosing to destroy the ship, because there wasn't any way for him to rig a self-destruct. The ship had one, but it slagged after that pulse ripped the shit out of them. Fusion reactors wouldn't overload, and the antimatter controllers refused to initialize.

It was simply a decision to give up and run, and then pray for a rescue that didn't involve becoming a pirate sex toy.

Accepting the inevitability of what he had to do, he blew out his cheeks in a long hissing sigh. "Do the passengers have some kind of command stack? Shit, do we have any coordination between us? At all?"

"Not directly," the handler said, pushing himself off the bench and shaking his head to clear what looked like a wave of pain. He bent over to pick up his pistol and checked the charge clip before he stuffed it into his holster. "I might not be much use in a fight, but I can carry a message."

"We've got no comm with these screaming-crazy-buttload-of-people?" Willis asked. "I don't want to send you out there, but we need to tell them it's time to vacate."

"Is this one of their commsets?" The medic who had been

treating the handler walked back up and held out a small box and an earpiece.

"Yah, that's one of theirs," the handler confirmed. "Where'd you get it?"

He nodded over at a body shrouded by a utility tarp. It was one of many laid in a row under the single covering. "She was carrying it. I didn't recognize her, so I assumed she was a passenger who ended up in the crossfire. Maybe she was one of their screaming crazy fighters."

He took it and stared at it for several seconds. Other than the earpiece, it was strange. It was a lot bulkier than the miniature comm units the crew routinely used on the ship, but he shrugged. *Just so it works.*

Putting it over his ear, he punched the button. A brief burst of static told him there was quantum level encryption on the system and he smiled. *Maybe not so backwards after all.*

"Unrecognized user. Log in, or state your identity," a voice said in his ear. He couldn't be sure it was human or artificial since it was barely audible.

"What?"

The voice came back louder. "Voice print identification in progress. Please confirm your identity." Willis still couldn't tell if it was human.

"This is Chief Engineer Jason Willis. I'm trying to reach someone in charge of the passenger... militia?"

"Confirmed. Engineer Willis. This is Solo."

"I need to talk to someone in charge. I want to give the order to abandon ship and I need to make sure your people know it's time to retreat."

"Understood. I am passing the word now," Solo said. "Our people are in position to cover your exit. We have control over transverse access corridor four, from Main Engineering down to

Portside Lifeboat Bay-2. How many crewmembers are with you in engineering?"

"Twenty-one crew, but we've been taking in casualties. I don't know how many injured we have."

The medic glanced over at him from where he'd started treating another handler with an oxygen concentrator tube. He held up seven fingers.

"Acknowledged. You have twenty-eight in your company," Solo said before he could relay the information.

"How do—"

"I have access to the optic directly above your position. We will prep lifeboats P-27 through P-30 for you."

"Do you have any idea how bad the O2 levels are outside of engineering?" he asked. He was watching the medic hold the concentrator up to the handler's face.

"Based on observational data, I estimate the oxygen level is between nine and thirteen percent. While this is not dangerously low for a short exposure, it will make physical exertion difficult. Distributing the load of your casualties across as many individuals as possible would minimize the impact and increase your chances of making it to the lifeboats."

"Understood. What about your people?"

"We are currently loading medical staff and critical care patients into lifeboats in the starboard bays and are prepared to launch concurrent with your departure. Please proceed quickly so we may commence operations to cover the lifeboat's withdrawal from the engagement area."

"Cover our withdrawal? Are there other ships out there?"

"Not at this time," Solo said.

"Then how the frak are you going to keep the pirates from sweeping us up?"

"To be blunt chief Willis, I do not have time to explain the details of our plan, but you must proceed immediately to your designated lifeboat. As it will require more than eleven minutes to load up your casualties and make it to the bay, you need to move now. It is imperative that you be clear of the blast radius within twenty minutes."

Blast radius?

CHAPTER TWENTY-FOUR

IT WAS ONLY A CHANGE in smell that told Kylla she was on N'gabo's ship. They had managed to make their first objective. Now to figure out what came next.

She kept her eyes closed and tried to inventory her surroundings as she clawed her way back toward consciousness. She wasn't alone. There was at least one other person near her. She could hear it breathing shallowly. It was still alive, but apparently not conscious either.

She drew in a breath slowly. Cautiously. Tasting the air.

Whoever it was that pressed against her, she could tell it wasn't an Augment. It was also female and vaguely familiar. *Probably Santore*, she decided.

Straining, she could hear muffled voices above the hiss of air ventilators. They echoed hollowly in the distance. *At least we're alone.*

Her senses came back first, but she still had almost no motor control, and no feeling of touch. Everything was gross mass and immovable objects.

This doesn't feel like the after affects of a stunner round. It was much deeper and more painful. *Maybe they hit us with a stunstick to make sure we stayed down?*

Summoning all her physical will, she managed to open one eye. The light was glaringly bright, but she could make out a wall of pink and brown that blocked most of her vision.

What the frak?

Forcing her other eye to open and to focus, she struggled to confirm what she was seeing. It took several seconds to recognize it.

That's skin. A breast. And at close range. She took a painful breath as she realized what that meant.

Frak! Frak! Frak! We've been strip searched. She hauled in another breath and tried to move her arm. Anything. She needed to know if they'd stripped them both.

Her own hand flew up in front of her face and crashed onto one of Santore's squishy parts.

"Get your hands off my tatties," the ExO hissed. Her voice sounded like she'd consumed way too much alcohol, but her meaning was obvious.

"Quiet," Kylla whispered. "We're on N'gabo's ship."

"Yah, I figured that out myself," she said. "But I feel like I've had too much party, and my brain is rattling in my skull."

"Am I naked?"

"Yah. Way too much party. I think I'm looking at your belly button," she confirmed.

"And I'm looking at someone's ass," Klinestrom mumbled.

Santore growled. "Close your eyes, Helmsman."

"Too late," he said.

"We've got a problem. I think they strip searched us."

"I think that's the least of our issues." Santore rocked over onto her back.

"Fuck get off my face!" he gasped.

"Well, now you know whose ass it was, don't you," she said.

Kylla flopped onto her back and squinted up at the ceiling.

"No, we have a real problem. I was carrying a thinpad. If they left it behind, I don't know how we're going to take over the ship." She ran her hands up over her body. "Damn. It's gone."

"Unless you know thinpad-jitsu, how were you going to take over a ship with only a thinpad?" Santore asked. She was pushing herself up onto her elbows.

Shaking her head to clear the fog that clung to the edges of her mind, Kylla rolled up to a sitting position, and tugged at her ear. "Just because we're alone, doesn't mean we're not being watched."

"I don't like not knowing what's going on," she said, pushing herself back against the wall beside Klinestrom.

He was staring down into his own lap and trying not to look at anything. Fortunately for him, Kylla's pheromones weren't anywhere near as strong as a full Augment, and his mortification was apparently outweighing what effect they might have had. So far.

"We're in a holding cell of some kind," she said. "I can tell that N'gabo's not interrogating Dorran or the others yet. She's talking to someone else."

"How do you know that?" Klinestrom asked, glancing up briefly.

"I can hear her voice."

"I can't hear shit," Santore said. "I need to know what the frak you got us into."

"I had tools on that thinpad that would have helped us take over her ship," she said.

"Access codes?" she asked, frowning. "That's not going to get us far against armed pirates."

"Yah I know, but she's not a pirate. She's a Hound," Kylla said.

"What's the difference?"

"She's a freelance hunter who contracts with the Institute to clean up problems. She's a lot more dangerous."

"How do you know that's what she is?" Klinestrom asked.

"The thing she hit the *Aggie* with was Shan Takhu technology, and I'd be willing to bet that isn't the only gear she's packing either. We probably came aboard through a jump door," she said. "Plus, I know who she is. She has a reputation."

"What the hell does that mean, and what does it get us," Santore asked.

"Nothing yet. But if I can get out of this cell, maybe we can still turn this around."

"That's a polycon door. It looks like it's remotely locked, too. Unless you've got superhuman strength in your bag of magic tricks, you're not breaking it down."

"I know," she said, pushing herself up to a standing position. Klinestrom blinked and she could see his skin start to flush as he looked her over.

Damn it. We don't need him distracted and losing it.

"You won't understand this, but you can't control your reaction," she explained, putting it out there so he had a fighting chance. "My pheromones are a byproduct of my genetic augmentation. It's not intentional, but you'll just have to deal with it until we get out of here."

"Genetic augmentation?"

"Yah, she's a plusser, so keep your eyes down, Mr. Klinestrom. Otherwise she'll melt your brain," Santore said. Unfortunately, she was also showing signs of the same hormonal response.

He snorted his disbelief but took her advice, anyway.

"If I had my thinpad, we'd already be out of here," she said, trying to keep them focused on what they needed to be addressing. "I wonder if they took it from me before we got to her ship, or after?"

Suddenly her optic vibrated against her bicuspid.

Solo!

It was apparently monitoring her recording channel.

Now to figure out how to use that.

She scanned the corners of the room before she knelt down, facing away from the door. Tilting her head to make sure she had Santore's attention she reached up and ran her finger around the hole in her cheek and then pointedly wagged the optic with her tongue.

The ExO stared at it for a second, then nodded.

"If we had the thinpad, we could communicate. In binary if nothing else."

"Yes and No?" Santore added, nodding that she understood Kylla was communicating to someone else through her optic.

"Exactly."

Her tooth vibrated once, and she winked, letting Santore know that she had comm with someone.

"What would you do if you had it?" she asked, leading the conversation in a direction so that Kylla could put questions out there without being obvious.

"I'd try to see if we could get out of here, but I think I need that thinpad to do it."

Two short pulses. *No?*

Behind her, the door latch clicked. She jumped up and spun to look at it, expecting to see someone coming in. It didn't move.

She glanced over her shoulder and both Santore and Klinestrom were on their feet. He wasn't looking at the door, and she shook her head. "Eyes down," she whispered.

Santore smacked the back of his head and chuckled at his obvious mortification.

The door clicked twice. And then twice more, before her tooth buzzed again. Once. *Yes?*

"I don't know," she said. "Maybe the thinpad's not that

important after all?"

One more buzz. *Yes*.

She stepped up to the door and gently wiggled it. It was unlocked.

Solo was obviously in the ship's computer system. Somehow, even if the thinpad hadn't made it over, it had managed to take over the *Seeker*'s AA.

"I think we're good. It's unlocked," Kylla said, grinning as she looked back at them. The helmsman was glaring at the wall intensely.

"Are we safe to talk?" Santore asked, glancing up at the corner of the room where she apparently assumed the surveillance optics would hide.

One buzz. She nodded.

"What the hell is happening?"

"We needed to get my AA inside N'gabo's ship," she said. "Apparently that's happened in spite of them strip searching us."

Her tooth vibrated a steady long pulse.

"I get it. You used my optic recording channel to upload your distribution code?" she asked.

Yes.

Klinestrom shot her a very brief questioning eyebrow since she'd unexpectedly included someone else in the conversation who wasn't in the room.

Santore just nodded.

"The AA we had in our lab is part of an extremely sophisticated Distributed Awareness with over 130 years of experience," she explained. "It also contained some features that we can't really talk about, but it was designed to overwrite AA systems."

"You're talking about Odysseus?" Klinestrom asked.

"No, but it's similar in some ways," she said. "Odysseus was destroyed in the battle of L-4 Prime, but one instance of the self-replicating Distributed Awareness code survived in a lab. The Dutch AA that runs the human side of the Shan Takhu Archive in Zone One modified Solo to be safe."

"I'm not sure I like how that sounds," Santore said. "That kind of technology nearly destroyed civilization."

The helmsman was nodding at the wall behind her.

"We can debate the ethics of Solo's existence later," she said. "Right now, what matters is that it's working with us, and has apparently already infiltrated N'gabo's ship. Let's see what we can do to turn this around, shall we?"

"Can we look into maybe finding me some pants first?" he asked, turning to face Kylla with a pained expression that made it hard not to laugh at his discomfort.

Santore glanced over at him, and then downward. "Yah, I think he needs to get that under cover before it grows its own brain."

"Too late," he hissed as his blush threatened to split his blood supply even further.

CHAPTER TWENTY-FIVE

WHEN THEY CAME ABOARD, the muscle boys locked Dorran in a small holding room with the three T-r Series Augments. They hauled the unconscious bodies of Kylla and the others off to another section of the ship, and there'd been no sign of what happened to them. But after the generous application of stunstick tenderization, they probably wouldn't be awake anytime soon, anyway.

As they waited for N'gabo to argue out some kind of deal with the other pirate captains for control of the Creche, Tia repeated every word of the negotiations for his benefit.

He had augmented vision, and strength, and increased synaptic density, but the T-r Series Augments had the full kit. As he sat and listened to Tia, he had to admit that given their situation, better ears would have been a useful upgrade.

"They're done," Tia said, opening her eyes and staring at the door. She was perspiring like she'd been running the treadwheel for hours, but her eyes had taken on a hollowness that said she was heading for trouble. She was burning way too much energy to keep moving for much longer.

"Are you alright?" he asked, wondering how much time any of the three of them had without renormalizing their metabolism.

It couldn't be a lot.

"Here they come," one of the others said. Unlike Tia, neither of them had chosen names yet. Dorran called them Other One and Other Two in his mind.

The three of them stood up slowly. They were all borrowing energy from pure adrenaline.

Dorran waited until Anders unlocked the door and gestured for them to come out. He looked at the three newborns, all sweating.

"Life support out in there?" Eddington asked as they filed past.

"Dono," Dorran said with a shrug. "Felt fine to me."

"What's wrong with them?"

"I don't think they've had firstmeal," he said. "Maybe they're just dying of starvation." It was terribly close to true, even though none of them would admit it.

When they followed Anders onto the back riser of the ConDeck, it was clear that N'gabo was unhappy with how things went in her negotiations. When the deal ironed down, apparently their Creche technology was worth more to her than all the rest of the ship, since Tia had reported she'd offered them enough chit to buy a small planet.

Even with what he lacked as an empathic reader, Dorran knew she wouldn't be happy with putting out the extra investment. And that frustration was likely going to be aimed in their direction.

N'gabo stood on the lowest level of the small ConDeck staring out the forward viewscreen as they filed in. There was nothing visible but stars, not even the *Agamemnon*. Obviously, when they'd walked through the jump door, they'd covered more klicks than he could believe.

Like Anders said, it was a very long walk.

But only a single step.

"I really dislike having to change my plans," N'gabo said, without turning to face him. He could see her face reflected off the screen and knew she was watching him. She had the same kind of intensity that Kylla showed when she was reading expressions.

Maybe she's not a true telepath?

"I'm not fond of it either," Dorran agreed, as he struggled to bite back on his sarcastic first impulse. "I was planning on retiring on—"

"I do not need you to tell me your plans, Mr. James," she said, turning in his direction. She held her hands behind her back as she stepped closer and studied his eyes. "You do know that you can't keep anything from me. I will know your plans."

"Other than retirement, I don't think I had anything set in granite," he shrugged. "And I'd wager those ideas are probably changing at this point."

"Indeed," she agreed, leaning closer and wrinkling her nose. "Unless your desire was to spend your days in a fifteen cubic meter box. Runaway plussers don't get much in the way of accommodations in Dziban."

"Is it sunny there?" he asked. "I can adapt."

She rolled her eyes. "You're interesting, but I think I'll come back to you when I'm done with them. I am sure you have much to share with me."

"I don't think so," he said. "Coffee, maybe? If you're buying. My retirement fund—"

Anders jammed him up against the bulkhead with the butt of his rifle as N'gabo turned her attention toward Tia.

"Careful, she's fast," he warned, clicking the safety off on his stunner.

N'gabo nodded and waved his comment away without looking in his direction. "She's triple bound and exhausted. I doubt she's that dangerous."

"I wouldn't wager my eggs on that," Carmichael said. He'd also unlocked his safety and stepped down onto the main floor. It gave him a better line if he needed to react to anything. And more distance.

She shook her head. She was staring into Tia's eyes. "You are the newborn one?"

"We are," she said, rocking her head to include the two other T-r Augments. "And you are N'gabo? The telepath?"

"You've heard of me?"

"No."

Eddington snorted. Once. The reaction he got from N'gabo was enough that he knew he'd pay dearly for his brief amusement. He swallowed whatever other noise he may have been contemplating and focused on the end of his rifle.

"I pay attention, plus I was warned you're a contact telepath."

"I am," she said. "That means I can pull what I want to know out of your mind. You won't be able to keep secrets from me. Does that frighten you?"

"Not particularly," Tia said. "Does it frighten you?"

N'gabo laughed, raising an eyebrow as she drew in a deep breath. "She's definitely a recent emergence. She still stinks like fluorocarbon."

"Well, if you want to give me a minute, I can go freshen up," she said, smiling innocently.

"And she hasn't learned to hold her tongue," Anders added.

Shaking her head, N'gabo never broke eye contact. "That's typical. They emerge with all the knowledge they can cram into their brains with their direct synaptic training, but they've got no life experience."

"Sounds like most Doctorates I've ever known," Anders said.

"You actually know smart people?" Tia asked, looking at him

with doubt.

"Oh, you are definitely crafted of finer cloth, Newborn," N'gabo said. "It will be a real shame to cut you up to see if we can figure out your genome."

"Right. About that? Were you going to get around to your mind-reading-séance-voodoo thing before the kids fall asleep over there? It's way past their naptime," Dorran said. He could tell that Anders didn't do well with having his eggs stomped in front of his men. The way his jaw flexed as he stood there with a lethal weapon in his hand, there was no doubt that if it went on much longer, his rage issues would overpower his discipline.

"They only need a sample and not dissection to determine that kind of thing," Tia said with a slight shrug. "If you had more smart people in your universe, you'd probably know that."

"Enough of the banter, Newborn," N'gabo said, the amusement in her face sublimating to a frosty cloud, as something much more intense and sinister took over.

She brought her hand around from behind her back and peeled a thin black glove off her fingers. Dorran stared, trying to focus on boosting his visual acuity. It looked like there was something *technological* attached to the palm of her hand, but he couldn't be sure.

Reaching up, she took Tia's face between her hands and closed her eyes. She tilted her head forward in concentration, but after several seconds, she dropped her arms and stepped back, shaking her head.

She would have stumbled off the riser except that Anders stopped her with an outstretched arm. "Did you get what you needed?" he asked.

N'gabo blinked several times and her eyes looked like molten glass.

"She did not," Tia answered for her. "She couldn't keep up."

"You've never tried that with an Augment that hasn't been metabolically renormalized, have you?" Dorran asked. "Was it painful?"

She focused on him but didn't answer.

"We can save some time and a brainache for you," he offered. "Even with whatever Institute magic you've got glued to your hand, the three of them are all still running at twenty times the normal synaptic rate. They all emerged from their Incubators without the normal processing. So, they'll pretty much burn your brain out trying to keep up."

She nodded.

"And with me, you won't have that kind of problem, but I don't know what any of the plans were. Kylla kept me in mushroom mode so I couldn't tell you what she wanted to do."

"You can't take it for granted that he's telling the truth," Anders said.

"No problem," he said, stepping forward and smiling. "You can probe me all you want, but I have one question. I've heard telepathy is intimate... like sex. Does that mean I get to enjoy it?"

CHAPTER TWENTY-SIX

KYLLA STARED AT THE SMALL SCREEN at the end of the hall. They were in some kind of cell block, but there were no other occupants. Nor were there any guards.

She could still hear conversations through the ventilation ducts, but the ship sounded mostly empty.

"Solo are you able to access the internal comm?" she asked.

The screen in front of her blinked. "Yes, I have access to all ship systems."

"Excellent."

"Unfortunately, I can access none of the non-human technologies," it added.

"Did they bring the thinpad over and leave it open?" she asked. It would have been a critical mistake if they'd found it and then brought it along. Her plan was that they wouldn't have found it until after they got over.

"In fact, they did leave it behind," he said. "I anticipated that possibility and used your optic as a secondary infiltration channel," It said. "I apologize that I had to overwrite your personal device to achieve our objective, however the memory of the unit was insufficient to—"

"Worry about it later," she said. "What's the status."

"Nandia N'gabo is currently on the ConDeck with four security handlers and our people. There is a single engineer and one other person aboard the *Seeker*. All other crewmembers are actively involved in trying to secure the Creche equipment from the *Agamemnon*."

"No one else is aboard this ship?" Santore asked.

"Negative," Solo said.

"What about the *Aggie*?" she asked. "Who is still there?"

"Within another few minutes none of your crew, or any passengers, will remain on the *Agamemnon*. We will have safely evacuated everyone who is left alive."

"That won't last long," Klinestrom said. "They'll just scoop up the lifeboats and pods." He'd looked in all the open cells but had given up his quest for clothes and stood behind them trying to count ceiling panels.

Kylla shook her head. "We can't let them take the Creche technology."

"I have intercepted communication that indicates they brokered a new deal for access to the cargo holds and passenger wards. N'gabo promised the pirates the cargo and hardware in exchange for assistance in capturing you and your staff. However, since they now know what we were carrying, she does not want them to take control of it."

"That sounds like her style," she said. "They came to terms?"

"It appears they have done so," Solo said. "A large capital investment seems to have motivated the pirate captains to capitulate."

"How long do we have?"

"Unknown, but because they do have a jump door system on the *Seeker*, it will not take long to disassemble the Creche components and transport it out of the *Agamemnon*."

"They have seven people on this ship, and there are seven of us, assuming that N'gabo brought everyone over," Kylla said. "We need to move quickly."

"I hate to keep repeating myself, but I don't want to get into a fight without pants," Klinestrom said.

"There is a garment printer in engineering," Solo offered. "It is located one deck up and aft. However, the two bodies I mentioned previously are stationed there. One is watching conventional ship systems, and the other is at the jump door controller."

"That means that at least one of them is an Augment or Institute modified," she said. "You might be over your air supply trying to take them."

"And they're probably better armed than we are," Santore said. "Especially being naked and all that." She glanced over at the helmsman and added, "Well maybe not him. He's pretty well armed."

"How are our children doing?" Kylla asked, swallowing a laugh, and trying to drag Santore out of her own spiraling hormonal funk.

"They are currently unharmed, although the T-r Series Augments are starting to show evidence of physical fatigue."

"Once we take the ship and get to safety, we can deal with that," she said. "Where are they?"

An image from the ConDeck appeared on the screen. "N'gabo has not had the opportunity to use her abilities fully. As you expected, the T-r Series Augments are resistive to her telepathic skills. So far she does not seem to know anything that would prevent us from accomplishing our goals."

"It looks like there are only four hardbodies providing cover," Santore said. "If we can distract them, we might be able to pull off a first strike."

"That might be easy for the two of you," Klinestrom said.

"Just open the door and say hi."

"I doubt it," Kylla said, looking back at him and winking. He was obviously suffering in a huge way. "They're trained Hounds. They'll be used to dealing with the pheromone fog, and if not, I'll guarantee N'gabo has them plugged and filtered."

"Yah, but... nevermind." He shrugged. "What the hell is this hormone thing? Is it a weapon or something?"

"It was originally an accident, and they never figured out how to fix it," she said. "The closest explanation I heard was that it's evolutionary nature that positive mutations to the genome want to succeed. That means the drive to reproduce more aggressively is inherent in dominant genetic design."

Shaking her head, Santore frowned. "Fascinating as that may be, my concern is that we're still unarmed and naked, and we need to get something happening."

"The idea of a well-timed distraction isn't bad," she said. "Solo, can you swing something into place?"

"Even if we get the initiative, we're not packing the right weapons to take them down. We need to fix that," she said.

"If we can get a message to Tia, they should easily be able take out the soldiers," Kylla said. "I wonder how good their ears are?"

"What?" Santore asked.

"Their ears should be better than mine, and I can almost make out what they're saying through the air ducts," she explained.

"Biscuits," she said, pulling her mouth sidewise in a sarcastic sneer.

She nodded. "That's how I knew the ship was almost empty. Watch the screen," she said, walking over to the nearest ventilator. Without raising her voice, she said, "Tia, this is Kylla. If you can hear me raise your right hand."

On the screen, the Augment scanned the room looking for the optic. She turned enough to show her hands were still bound, but she raised her right shoulder several inches instead.

"I'll be frakked," Santore said, shaking her head in disbelief.

"That's a little scary," Klinestrom added. He was obviously struggling to keep up with the shifts in his reality, but pieces kept dropping into place through the fog. Finally, he shook his head. "I thought you were dragging me out, but you really are a plusser? Like her?"

"Not exactly," she said. "I'm a prototype from before we figured out how to build ones like her."

"Yah, she's older than your great-grandmother," Santore said, laughing as he visibly wilted.

"I'll explain that when we have time, but we have other things to do now," Kylla said. "What can we do for a diversion?"

"Before we do anything, you must disable the jump door controller." Solo said.

"To keep them from bringing reinforcements back from the *Aggie*?" she asked.

"It is to protect the *Seeker*," it said, without further explanation.

"I assume this door controller is in engineering," Santore said, glancing at the helmsman.

He was still running a half minute out of phase, but he was gaining on reality. "Does that mean I can get some pants?" he asked.

Grinning at his sudden enthusiasm, Kylla turned to face the ventilator. "Tia, we've got to take a detour to engineering, and then we're on our way."

On the screen, she looked around to make sure no one was watching her and then nodded slowly.

"You'll have to get yourself free of those binders before we get there. Can you do it?"

She nodded again, holding up her right hand. Blood ran up her forearm from where the binder straps had cut in before she'd broken them.

"I was wrong before. That's really scary," Klinestrom whispered as he rubbed the marks on his wrists from where they'd been bound.

"What's the distraction?" Santore asked as Kylla spun and trotted for the lift at the opposite end of the cellblock. She and Klinestrom dropped in behind her.

Solo followed along on the audio pickups in the overhead. "The lifeboats have already achieved a minimum safety margin. Once you disconnect the jump doors, I believe a three gigaton antimatter detonation will be an adequate distraction."

Behind her, she heard Santore slow down as she realized what they were going to do, but to her credit, she never quit moving.

CHAPTER TWENTY-SEVEN

TAKING ENGINEERING WAS easier than they expected. They had no strategy but surprise, and thankfully it worked.

Three naked people charging in, just as the lights went out, was enough of a non-sequitur that with the help of a couple flying body blows and some loud screaming, it was over almost as fast as it had started.

When the lights came back on, Santore was sitting on top of the engineer's stomach pummeling him to unconsciousness with her fists, and apparently enjoying herself a lot more than she should.

He was not going to be getting up anytime soon.

Kylla's target had vanished entirely, but since she'd aimed to knock him off the platform and into the machinery below, it wasn't a surprise that he was missing. Unfortunately, she'd almost followed him over the edge and dangled by one hand from the railing while she scanned for any other potential threats.

In spite of what Solo said, she was in no mood to take chances.

Fortunately, there was no one else around.

Looking down onto the lower engineering deck, ten meters below, she realized there was no possibility her target would be a problem. Ever again. His skull was not as durable as the reactor housing he'd tried to penetrate, with his face.

"I'm too old for this shit," she groaned as she hauled herself back onto the deck and walked toward Klinestrom.

He watched her and then glanced around, looking for the person she'd taken out. "Disintegrating death rays?" he asked. "I need to get me that kind of genetic upgrade."

"Gravity," she said, winking. "It works every time."

The helmsman started to head over to look, but she grabbed his arm and shook her head. "You don't want to do that. He's had a catastrophic disassembly."

Klinestrom opened his mouth to respond but decided there was nothing he needed to say.

"He's very dead," she confirmed.

"I think mine is, too," Santore said, standing up and grabbing the stunner he had in his holster. As she stepped back, she kicked him once for good measure and then cracked three rounds into him. She smiled as she watched him twitch for several seconds. Shrugging, she added, "Insurance."

"At least now we've got a gun," Klinestrom said.

"Yah, but we'll need to leave it here," Kylla said. She didn't look up and was fiddling with the otherwise featureless obelisk that her target had been working with.

"It's been a long time since I played with any of this tech. Too long." She shook her head.

"What is it?" Santore asked. Obviously confused by the fact that Kylla's hands had faded into the smooth surface almost up to her wrists.

"The door controller. It creates dimensionless bridges between two locations in space time."

They both stared at her blankly.

"It's how we came aboard," Kylla said, frowning as she pulled her hands out of it. "I closed all the doors, but I can't shut it down. One of us needs to stay here in case they have a remote activator."

"To close them again?" Santore asked, gingerly touching the device. When her hands didn't pass through it, she rapped her knuckles against its surface to confirm it was solid. "That would have to be you, since neither of us would even know where to begin."

"I have to help you take the ConDeck," she said. "Solo will know if her people start jumping back and Mr. Klinestrom can just shoot it with a stunner round or ten, to make sure it overloads."

"Why don't we just do that now and be done with it?" he suggested.

"All the Shan Takhu systems are linked to a separate power broadcast system. If we overload this one, it might cause all those pieces of hardware to go down and that would alert N'gabo that something's twisty. We only want to do that as a last resort."

"Fine, so you two get to go be warriors, and I'll just hang out. Maybe I'll print me some pants while I wait."

"If you're tired of hanging out, that's a good idea," Santore said, handing the pistol to him. "Me personally, I liked the shocked look on this guy's face before the lights went out."

She walked back over and kicked the engineer once more. He flopped over like a bag of wet protein. "What's next?"

"You need to proceed quickly," Solo said. "One of the pirate raiders is showing an interest in the fleeing escape pods."

"How much time do we have?" Kylla asked. She was already moving toward the door.

"If we want to catch the raiders in the blast, then we need to overload our reactor as quickly as possible."

"I was wondering how you planned to do that," Santore said as she followed her out the door and back to the lift. "I didn't think the *Aggie*'s antimatter stores were that big."

"They are not," Solo confirmed as it switched speakers to keep up. "One of the raiders is powering up its coils. You need to be on the upper deck in under thirty seconds to maximize the collateral effects of the diversion."

Stopping at the lift gate, she looked up at the ventilator opening above her head. "Tia, I am not where I can see you, but you have about thirty seconds before things go sidewise. As soon as you see shit start, you three go for the biggest threats first. And make sure you aren't facing a window."

Santore flung the gate open and jumped in, pulling Kylla after her by her arm. She hit the button for the top deck, and they oozed upward. The lift was painfully slow.

Without warning, the lights went out again.

"What the frak?" the ExO asked.

"I am improvising," Solo said.

Another voice came over the shipwide comm. "Intruder alert, we've got people in engineering."

"What's going on down there?" someone else said. It was a male voice, and his tone made it sound like he was in charge.

"I don't know but there are three people running around shooting things."

"Where did they come from?" a woman asked. Kylla recognized her voice as N'gabo. She sounded more amused than concerned.

"I don't know, they just appeared out of nowhere."

"Call a security team back from the *Agamemnon* to cover you," she said.

The lift stopped, and the gate opened. There was no light from anywhere, but Kylla could hear voices up ahead. They sounded like they were debating over what to do.

"There are two shallow alcoves to the left and right of the

main corridor, approximately ten meters ahead," Solo said as they leapt out into the dark. "The ConDeck still has full illumination so when they enter the hallway you will have the advantage of concealment."

"Is Klinestrom in trouble?" Santore asked.

"He is in no danger," Solo said. "I am the voice you are hearing from engineering."

"Shit, I am glad you're on our side," she whispered as they trotted forward while dragging their hands along the walls to find their spots.

"They've shot our ST Technician," Solo said in the other voice, even adding a touch of believable fear to his tone. "He's down. I don't know if the doors are working."

"Fuck this. I'm sending help," the one in charge snarled.

"Two men leaving the ConDeck," Solo warned quietly as they both dove into their hiding holes.

The door to the ConDeck opened and light flooded down the hall. It wasn't bright enough to see anything clearly, but after the total darkness, it outlined the soldier's silhouettes along the floor. Kylla pressed herself back into her hole as far as possible. Looking up, she realized that Santore had at least two features that stuck out far enough to be visible if they happened to look in the right direction.

"Power's down out here," one of the men said.

"Carmichael, are you afraid of the dark, too?" the leader said. "You've got handbeams. Move out."

"Yes sir," Carmichael said as the door closed, and the corridor fell back into darkness. Several seconds later two small circles of illumination flashed on and the men started forward. For the most part, they kept their beams on the floor while they advanced.

As they approached where the two of them were hiding, one

light flicked up and caught a glint of pink skin. They both froze. "What the frak?"

Santore apparently decided to improvise as well. Stepping out into the hall, she began backing toward the lift. Their lights tracked her for almost a second before one of them growled. "Hold!"

She raised her hands but took another step back. And another one.

"I said hold!" he said, slipping past Kylla's alcove. He had his stunner in one hand and his light in the other. He was concentrating on keeping an eye on the naked woman and nothing else.

"It's Santore," the other one said as he stepped up and stopped right in front of Kylla. She held her breath. "How the hell did she get out of her cell?"

"I don't know, let's get her in straps then we'll figure it out," the one she recognized as Carmichael said, leaning forward and pointing his light at the ground. "On your knees."

"I don't think you're packing enough gear for me," Santore said sarcastically, but she bent forward like she was complying. "Nope. Not even from down here," she added.

"Shut your hole," he snarled, watching her squat down.

She wasn't kneeling. *She's loading for launch.*

The one standing in front of Kylla slipped his stunner into its holster loosely and reached back with the other hand to get the binder straps out of his pouch.

Kylla stepped out of the dark, snagging his stunner and spinning out into the open behind the man. She rattled off two shots into the back of his legs. He hit the floor like a bag of recycler biscuits.

Santore uncoiled from her crouch and knocked Carmichael into the air hard enough he slammed into a ceiling bulkhead. He hit the ground flat on his face and Kylla finished him off with a stunner pellet to his neck.

Unfortunately, their attack wasn't remotely quiet, and the door to the ConDeck flew open. Several stunner rounds ricocheted down the hall blindly.

Kylla dropped to the floor and returned fire, but Santore wasn't as quick. She took a glancing blow to her arm and howled as the neuro-shock tore through her. Collapsing against the wall, she swore in at least a dozen languages, as she fought to swallow the agony and stay on her feet.

The one firing at them wore body armor, and even though Kylla hit him several times in the torso, he didn't go down. Though it didn't matter since Tia flashed into position behind him and slammed his head against the door seal repeatedly. He made several crunching noises before she dropped him to the floor.

The sucking gurgle as he fought to draw in his last breath made it clear he wouldn't get back up.

Kylla hurled herself up and charged toward the door as the lights on the ConDeck behind the Augment went out. She knew there was still another soldier up there, and the hissing crack of stunner rounds told her he was fighting back.

"Solo. Now!" she hollered as she watched a round catch Tia squarely between the shoulder blades.

Several seconds later the flash of the Agamemnon's death was brilliant and glaring. As stunning as the antimatter explosion was, it wasn't what held her attention. Silhouetted against the glare of the blast, she watched as Tia turned and shook off the stunner round. She walked straight back against at least two more rounds without flinching.

Another crunch of bones ended the fight.

The Seeker was theirs.

CHAPTER TWENTY-EIGHT

"Don't kill her," Kylla said quietly into the silence. One of the T-r Augments had N'gabo hanging fifteen centimeters off the deck by her neck. She was flailing wildly and clawing at his arms as she gasped for air.

He shrugged, and eased her back to the floor, obviously releasing some of the grip he had on her throat. But not all of it.

"Why Not?" Dorran asked, tilting his head to the side as he looked the two women over. He'd dropped down into one of the pilot's seats and was smiling. "And while I'm asking questions, why are you both naked?"

"Camouflage," Santore said, shrugging. She was staring out the window and watching the dying glow of the *Agamemnon*.

"They strip searched us, and we haven't had a chance to find our clothes," She corrected. "And I think Santore's decided she likes the Amazon Warrior look."

Dorran nodded. "She wears it well."

The gesture she flung in his direction had minimal impact, but he did wink. "No disrespect, ma'am."

She probably didn't notice.

"How did you get out of your cell?" N'gabo asked. She was still struggling to breathe.

"Same way we took your ship. I've got a smarter AA than you do." Kylla shook her head, and the Augment eased up again.

"What?"

"Whoever strip searched us missed something." She flicked her optic with her tongue and smiled.

Dorran laughed. "Distributed Awareness kicks ass again."

Kylla shot him with her best glare. *Shut the hell up.*

"Oops," he said quietly.

"We don't have time to discuss this now," she said, nodding at the engineer. "Take her down to deck four and lock her up."

"Why don't you just vent her?" Santore suggested, tearing her eyes away from the view. The explosion had almost faded entirely, and she was shaking her arm as she tried to get some feeling back into it.

"I'd be good with that," Dorran agreed. "Even the brain sex wasn't that great."

N'gabo snorted, but the hand around her throat twitched, cutting her off before she could reply.

"We'll need her later. She knows things I have to find out. When we've got time, we'll dig them out of her." Kylla dropped into the seat beside the engineer and let out a long, slow breath. "We're not done yet."

He still looked skeptical, but he stood up and waved toward the door. "After you."

"Take the boys and drag the two in the hall along with you. Put them in separate cells and make sure you don't touch her. I don't want her getting another chance to read you."

"She's got a thing on her hand she uses to read minds," Dorran said. "Some kind of tool." He reached out and snagged her thumb and twisted it around, bending her palm back painfully.

"What is it?" Kylla asked, leaning forward to look at it.

"It's an *Urah Un*," N'gabo said, shrugging. "It doesn't give me the ability. That's in my genetics. It amplifies what I already have. It also makes it less painful for those I read."

"*Urah Un*? Hand of the Ancient Ones." Kylla translated the Shan Takhu words. Reaching out and touching it with a fingertip, she watched it let loose of N'gabo's hand and curl up like a dead spider.

"If you won't let me touch her, how can I strip search her?" Dorran stuck out his lower lip and looked like he intended to cry. "I miss out on all the fun."

Santore laughed. "It's only fair, you know," she said.

"Alright, you can do that," she said, winking as she delicately took the *Urah Un* and put it on the console beside her. "But be thorough. I don't want you missing anyplace she might have something else like this hidden."

"Got it, she's dangerous and slick."

"When you're done with your brain sex, make sure you get your shots, and then head down to engineering. There are a couple uglies to clean up, and we need Klinestrom up here. Fast as."

"See, there you go again. Giving me the biscuit work." He bent down and picked up a stunner from one of the two soldiers on the floor. Using it as a prod, he nudged N'gabo toward the door.

"Now what?" Santore asked as she shoved one of the bodies out into the hall so she could close the door behind them.

"Solo, what's our status?"

"I have control of all ship's systems. We are standing by for your orders."

"What about out there?" Kylla waved toward the window.

"All three of the pirate raiders were destroyed in the explosion. One of the two that arrived with N'gabo's fleet is critically damaged," it said, superimposing a tactical display on the forward view. "Likely they will scuttle it when they are evacuated."

"Has anyone sent out a distress call?" Santore asked.

"Not at this time," it said. "The *Seeker* has been jamming all deep-comm since before we were brought aboard, and thus far, they are unaware that we have taken control."

"We need to finish them before they start picking off the lifeboats," Santore said. "The *Seeker* may have some special toys, but it's barely above a scout class. There's no way we can defend them all if they manage to get reinforcements."

Kylla shook her head. "We'll destroy any hostiles left, but we can't stay here more than a few hours," she explained. "We need to run."

"Run?" Santore crashed into the seat beside her, shocked that they wouldn't stay. The console behind her lit up, but she didn't look at it. "Why are we running?"

"Because the Shan Takhu Institute has the *Tahrat Shan-che*," she explained. "Last time I was on that ship, it was unarmed, but humans like guns, so by now they could have turned it into a battleship."

"But it's not anywhere around here," she said. "We were scanning two light years out before… uhm, before the fighting started."

"Not good enough," Kylla said. "Imagine an invisible ship that can leap interstellar space instantly, with jump doors that can deliver people across interplanetary distances, and that uses a spinning singularity to produce power."

"That sounds like bad tri-vid fiction." She snorted. "Or a paranoid delusion."

"You think so?" she said. "You stood in engineering and watched me operate the door controller. What did you see?"

"I'm not sure," she admitted. "It looked like an illusionist trick or a holographic projection, but I'll concede it was odd."

"Now imagine an entire ship, full of technology so advanced it would look like magic," she said. "It's not something you want to tangle with."

"What other stuff can it do?"

"Just take the jump doors," she said. "Imagine a door opening on this ship anywhere and a small antimatter mine rolling onto the deck."

"That would be bad," she said.

"And we've got one of those on the ship we just stole. Do you think they're going to let us keep it?"

"Probably not."

"When they show up to take it from us, they won't leave anyone out there alive to be a witness." She waved her arm out the window toward where the *Aggie* had been. "That's why I need you and Klinestrom to get us up on big, long legs as soon as you can."

Santore swung around to study the displays on the console behind her.

"Assuming you can fly this thing?"

"I thought you were the one going to drive," she said.

"I've flown the *Tahrat*. Over a century ago," Kylla said. "Most of the *Seeker* is human tech. I don't know if I could even get it moving."

"The controls are odd, but I think we can handle it," she said. "But we can't abandon the survivors to this monster ship when it gets here."

"Their best chance of survival is if we lead the *Tahrat Shanche* away."

"The what?" Klinestrom asked as he pushed the door open and shook his head. Apparently, his coveralls reinforced the fact that they were both still naked.

"It's the Shan Takhu ship that the Institute has," Santore said.

"I've heard of it," he said. "It ended the Odysseus War. That's ancient history."

Kylla rolled her eyes in his direction. Her glare melted him to the point that he probably forgot she was naked.

"What?" he asked as he wilted behind Santore's chair.

"I was there," she said. "It was me flying the *Tahrat*. And before you call me a liar, look it up."

"She did say she was 141," Santore confirmed.

"You weren't joking?" he asked. "My great grandmother is only 106."

She pushed herself up, grabbing the *Urah Un* off the console as she did. "Keep that in mind next time your hormones drag your mind sidewise little boy."

He squeaked as she reached out and ran a fingertip along his jawline.

"*Captain* Santore, the ship is yours," Kylla said. "You and Mr. Klinestrom need to familiarize yourselves with the controls so we can be ready as soon as we've figured out how the rest of this plays out."

"Yes, ma'am," she said, standing up and stepping aside so the helmsman could take the pilot's seat. She almost had to push him down physically, but it might have been because he was bending part of himself that shouldn't be bent.

"Do you want me to have them print you up a jumpsuit?" Kylla asked. "I can have somebody run it up here for you."

"I was thinking skin makes a good basic duty uniform," she said, winking as she stepped over and took her place at the other workstation. "It's kind of honest, don't you think, Klinestrom?"

"Yes, ma'am," he said quietly, scrunching his forehead into tight ravines and forcing himself to stare at the console.

"I need to call your attention to the physical condition of the T-r Series Augments," Solo interrupted. "They are all in critical need of medical attention."

Kylla spun toward where Tia had collapsed into one of the jump seats along the back of the ConDeck riser. Her eyes were vacant like she was barely conscious, and her hair hung in thick sweat-soaked mats against her head.

"What's wrong with her?" Santore asked.

"She is still running in an accelerated metabolic state," Kylla explained. "Augments age about twenty times normal for the first year of their lives. Usually we slow them down before they emerge from the Incubators, but these three weren't renormalized before we brought them with us."

"Is she going to be alright?" Klinestrom asked.

"Maybe," she said. "I'm not a doctor, and I don't know what we can do without one." Reaching out, she grabbed the Augment's wrist to check her pulse.

Tia jerked her arm away and Kylla looked down at her hand. Bright red blood covered her fingertips from where she'd snapped the binding straps. It surprised her that it was still fresh and oozing out, before she realized it had only been twenty minutes ago that they'd been in their cell.

It just felt like days.

"She is losing blood, but her priority is caloric intake," Solo said. "There is an automated care unit in the MedBay on deck three if you can get her there."

"Can you keep her alive?" Kylla asked as Santore jumped up to grab Tia. She shook her head, pointing back at the console.

"For now, with intensive intravenous nutrition," it said. "She expended substantially more energy than the other two T-r Augments, but they will rapidly fall into a similar condition without care."

Tossing Tia up onto her shoulder, Kylla asked, "How long?"

"A few days with metabolic inhibitors," Solo said. "Their

long-term survival will require genomic normalization."

"Can you do that?" she asked, as she ran down the hall toward the lift.

"If I had the proper medical files from the Creche," it said. "Unfortunately, the limited bandwidth of your optic channel forced me to prioritize awareness function over background information."

CHAPTER TWENTY-NINE

ADAM MICHAELS SAT alone in the forward compartment of the two-cabin lifeboat with his feet up on the seal edge of the observation window. Staring out at the black, he glared at the bright yellow star that dominated the view. It was the only thing interesting enough to look at, even though it was not much brighter than an average planet in the night sky of Mars.

It was barely a light-month away, but it was the only thing close enough to reach. That is, if they could figure out how to last almost a year at the best speed they could make in a lifeboat. He knew the seventh planet had a breathable atmosphere, but that was months beyond reach since they only had enough provisions for sixty days.

His boat might last double that since there were only four passengers aboard. Three Augments and a Mundane crewman from the *Agamemnon* who smelled like alcohol and sweat.

Four men who shared nothing in common except they shared a bubble of air, and an overwhelming sense of desperation.

He'd been listening to the chatter between the other survivors on the low gain comm. At first, he'd tried to coordinate some kind of plan, but eventually, reality had risen to the top of the debate, and the discussion devolved into something of a food fight. Because nobody had thought to build an adapting port so two lifeboats could tie together and share resources, the hard reality was that they were all on their own.

After the first hour, the only consensus they'd reached was that once anybody had a plan, they'd all stick together.

After that, he'd dialed down the comm and told the boat's small AI to filter the noise for things addressed specifically to him or their lifeboat ID.

It left him to sink deeper into his solitary contemplation of the star out the window. Unfortunately, his mind kept circling around the same idea.

There is no hope… if there is no rescue.

"What the fuck is that smell? Is something on fire?"

He snapped to his feet and spun toward the unexpected voice.

"Kylla?" He glanced over at the small instrument cluster on the overhead console to make sure the air recycler hadn't failed. "How the hell did you get here?"

She wrinkled her face. "Seriously, what the hell died in here?"

"We've got a stowaway," he said. "The pilot says it's the captain's spider monkey. Apparently, it's hiding in one of the ducts where we can't get to it to vent the damn thing."

She wrinkled her nose and blew out several fast breaths. "That's rough."

"I figure I'll eventually get used to it, but now that you're here…"

The expression on her face told him she was about to dump recycler biscuits on that hope. "You are here to rescue us, aren't you?"

She looked down and slowly shook her head. "Doctor… Adam. We can't."

"Why not?"

"That's complex, but it's for your own good," she said,

dropping into the jump seat beside where he'd been sitting.

He crashed down with her. "Alright let's say I can swallow that. Tell me what's going on."

"I got captured by a Hound."

"A slave hunter?"

"Yah, an Institute Operative. The top-deck-air-supply type," she said. "She also happens to be a one-of-a-kind Augment. A telepath."

"Nandia N'gabo?" he asked, raising an eyebrow almost to his hairline. "She was an anomalous recessive error. I didn't think she'd ever made it out of the Robinson Creche facility. You're saying she's hunting Augments now?"

"Not anymore," Kylla said. "We took her ship and have her locked down."

"You have her ship?"

She held up her hand before he could jump to any conclusion. "It's too small, and it's stuffed with Shan Takhu modifications. Which is what actually brought me here."

He shook his head.

"We need the normalization genomic codes for the T-r Series," she said. "I hope you saved your personal database."

He nodded. "I can do it."

She pulled out her thinpad and handed it to him.

"I have access to the *Seeker*'s robotic medical systems," Solo said through the thinpad's comm channel. "I can do the procedure manually if I can access the information I need."

"You're in the Creche," he said, scratching at his eyebrow and trying to get it to settle back to a normal position. "Why can't you access it from the main storage bank?"

"Actually, Solo is not in the core," she said, putting her hand on his knee. "And the Creche was destroyed with the *Agamemnon*."

He blinked several times as the reality bounced around in

his skill. Finally, he dropped his head into his hands and tried to breathe. He'd suspected as much, but he'd not internalized it yet. "It's probably better anyway," he said, fighting to accept the magnitude of their loss. Everything they'd worked on for a generation. Gone.

She set her hand on his shoulder and waited for him to get his grief pulled in. "We couldn't let the T-r Series fall into anyone's hands," she said. "That's why we need to have your records, Adam. We've kept the three T-r's that I took with me alive, but I need them normalized so they can help me run the *Seeker*."

"Sure," he said, starting to stand up and then thinking about it. "Why can't you take us with you."

"The Institute is going to come after us," she said. "They won't stop until they get us."

"Why?"

"I just jumped into a lifeboat 500 kiloklicks from where we're parked," she said. "There's absolutely no way they'll let that kind of tech out into the wild, and we haven't got a guess what other Shan Takhu toys she's got."

"Yah, they'll want it, won't they?"

"Which is why I need the file. I've got to get these two T-r's slowed down and back on their feet. Without them, I can't keep the Institute from dropping you all."

"I don't scan," he said, shaking his head.

"They're going to come hunting for the *Seeker*," she said. "We need to lead the *Tahrat Shan-che* away. If they catch us here, they'll leave no witnesses."

"They'll still catch you."

She nodded. "Probably, but the only hope you have will be if we're gone before they jump us. We're already on stolen time."

"You're going to leave us to drift?" He bit down on most of his exploding rage, but not before he pitched her thinpad at her.

"We'll tell the first merchant ship we run across where to find you. You just need to hang together until we can send help," she said. He could see in her eyes she didn't like the idea either, but that she also felt she had no other option. "A commercial carrier will have the resources to take you in. All we could do is bring a few of you aboard the *Seeker*, and then we'd all be dead before we made two parsec."

"That's bullshit," he hissed.

She nodded and stood up. The discussion was apparently over. "Here's the final calculus," she said. "We need your database, and I will be giving you one of the three T-r Augments I have with me."

"Why should we take one of them in?" He stared down at his hands and shook with rage. "All that'll do is shorten how long we can stay alive."

"Think this through. She's got the unnormalized genome," she explained. "That makes her a complete archive of the T-r Series genetic design. If you can keep her alive until you get rescued, you can restore your work."

"And if you resequence the ones you're keeping, they'll survive, but they won't be a pure record of the genome anymore." He nodded and stood up. Stepping toward the door to the back cabin, he stopped and shook his head. He knew he wasn't thinking square.

"How the fuck am I supposed keep her alive? This is a damned lifeboat, not a medical transport. All I've got are my hands and a first aid kit."

Kylla reached into her pocket and pulled out a small fob. She pressed her thumb into the end of it. "You might want to step out of the way," she said as Dorran's head appeared out of the wall.

"All clear?" he asked, winking at the doctor like it was normal to hang into a spaceship through the wall.

She nodded and a diagnostic bed slid out of empty space and bounced onto the floor. Stacks of supply crates tumbled through behind it. Adam jumped back out of the way and slammed against the cabin door.

"What the hell?" the Mundane crewman rumbled as he snatched the door open like he was looking for a fight. He stared in disbelief at the pile of stuff, glancing over his shoulder at the half empty bottle of rum on the small table, and apparently thinking he'd consumed more than he realized. "Where the frak did that shit come from?"

The doctor shook his head. "Baggage for our new passenger."

"New passenger?"

"Her," he said, as Dorran appeared again and carefully laid Tia on the table. Her wrists were wrapped in dressings, and bruises covered her arms and face. She smelled almost as bad as the monkey in the air duct.

Dorran grabbed a thick cable from under the bed and held it up. "Tie this into any power trunk and it will work. I gave you a set of universal couplers and programmed it with what we have on her current condition. Hopefully, you should be ready to stand it up."

"This is the best we can do," Kylla said, holding her hand out.

The doctor stared at her for several seconds before he realized what she was waiting for. He twisted around to grab his data server off the shelf above the bunk he called his. He looked at it in his hand and frowned. It was his whole life in a single archive. Every piece of work he'd ever done.

But so was the T-r Augment on the bed in front of him.

Finally, he let out a long, slow breath of air and held it out to her. "Do what you have to do."

"You just need to keep her alive until they find you," Kylla said. "We'll get help here as soon as we can."

"I know," he said, turning his attention to his new patient and not watching as she turned to leave.

The drunk snorted. "A lot of people died on the *Aggie*. What's so important about her?"

Kylla stopped half-way through the jump door. "She may not look like much to you, but she's Ammo in a war we didn't even know was coming, until today."

CHAPTER THIRTY

"*Mendoza* to Rescue Six. Walker, we've got another one for you to check. We're uploading your trajectory now. Range sixty-seven kiloklick."

"Copy that, *Mendoza*. That's a ways out there this time," he said, lining up the target on his sensors and punching in the heading. The stars drifted past the windows as the autonav brought him around and fired the small sublight engine on his shuttle. He watched the display calculate his travel time.

Twelve minutes. He frowned and pushed the throttle forward to bring his speed up. It recalculated. *Four minutes, thirty seconds.*

Not that it would probably matter, since the last six lifeboats they'd retrieved had all been floating coffins. Whatever had destroyed the *Agamemnon*, damaged a lot of them in the process. Lifeboats were fragile and known to develop microfractures after debris impacts from a blast. By the time the passengers knew that they were losing air, it was too late.

"That's better," he said out loud.

"You talking to yourself again, Ethan?" Chelcee said through the open hatch to the back compartment. The med-tech was so quiet that he'd forgotten she was back there.

"Always," he said. "It's why I volunteer to drive shuttles every chance I can. At least the arguments I have when I'm alone, are smarter."

"And you stand a slightly better chance of winning," she said, pausing long enough he thought the conversation was over. "I felt you kick it. Have we got a hot one?"

"Dono, but I just hate driving slow when I've got power to burn. Sooner we get done out here, the sooner we can find some other boring shit to do."

Space was big and travel times were long, so it was always a matter of dealing with boredom. Especially on a huge commercial hauler like the *Mendoza*. Stumbling into the *Agamemnon* rescue and recovery was one of the most interesting things they'd done in the twenty-six months he'd been aboard.

It had been over four weeks since that strange little scout ship blew past them like demons were on its ass. They claimed that pirates had run the *Aggie* to ground and there were almost a thousand survivors near 127 G Centauri.

But the whole story had a reek to it, and they almost let it go.

Fortunately, several weeks later their flight plan took them within a parsec of the reported location, and Captain Tindall decided they should take a look, just to be sure. They found the first lifeboat within hours, and the survivors confirmed the story the ship had told.

From there, it was just widening the pattern until they swept up the stragglers. Or the bodies.

"What have we got?" Ethan asked over his shoulder as they slowed to look over the lifeboat.

Agamemnon S-22.

"It looks like the rest of them," she said. His sensors only read electromagnetic and optical frequencies, but the med-station in back had a biometric sensor kit to play with. She leaned forward and looked through the front windows. "Is it showing power?"

"Sure is," he said, dialing up the optic and superimposing an infrared image on the corner of the window. "It's warmer than ambient. It might still have an atmosphere."

"Nothing says it's breathable," she pointed out. "But I might be reading life signs."

"Well, let's see if we get to be heroes today," he said, taking over manual control and swinging into a slow loop around the lifeboat.

There was no light visible coming through the forward window. "It's dark in there. That's not good." Of course, there were no view ports in the back cabin of a lifeboat, but it did look ominous.

"Yah, but look at the thermal," she said, leaning forward and pointing at the screen. "That looks to me like there's someone in the front compartment. Maybe they're sleeping?"

Tapping the searchlight on, he aimed it in the windows and eased forward to get a better view. Squinting to try to see anything past the reflective coating of the plasglass, it did look like there could be something. He could almost make out what looked like a medical diagnostic bed. And maybe someone asleep on it.

"That's not standard gear on a lifeboat," Chelcee said, jumping back into the rear compartment and grabbing her kit.

He nodded, punching in on the comm. "*Mendoza* Rescue Shuttle Six to *Agamemnon* lifeboat S-22. Do you copy?" He waited for several seconds, listening to the silence.

"Anything?" she asked, pausing while he scanned through the emergency channels.

"I'm not hearing anything," he said, keying the comm again. "Rescue Six to Lifeboat S-22. Do you copy? Hello? Anybody home?"

"Looks like we might have to suit up and do a hard entry," he said, angling up toward the hatch on the top of the boat.

"Wait!" she barked, jumping to point at the thermal image. "Movement."

He looked at the infrared screen again and nodded. The person on the bed was waving an arm feebly in their direction. A second later the lights came on in the cabin and two men squeezed through the door. One of them stopped to let the other one dive toward the control console.

"Hello? We see you. Hello, do you hear me?"

"Yah, this is Rescue Six. We copy." Ethan said. He could feel the relief and desperation in the man's voice. "Heard you might be looking for a ride?"

"We are so looking for a ride," he said, collapsing down in the seat. "We'd given up on ever being..."

"You've been out here a while," Ethan said. "How many of you are alive in there?"

"All of us," he said. "For now. Five and a half."

"Cool beans. Let me scoot up top and tie off." Ethan nudged them into position and lined up on the egress hatch.

"Do you need medical attention?" Chelcee asked, cutting herself in on the comm while he piloted.

"Four of us are fine, but we've got one with critical needs. I've got her deeply sedated, but she's got problems that we'll need to address."

"You've got her sedated? That's dangerous unless—"

"I'm a genetic surgeon," he interrupted. "The sedation is all that's kept her alive."

"Copy that," she said. "Do you have any special protocols for your patient? The *Mendoza*'s only a commercial hauler, but I can run it up the stack and have a triage team on standby."

"What she needs is a cryopod. You don't have one of those, do you?"

"Actually, we do," she said. "We're tooled for class five chem

187

loads, so we have a crit-care MedBay. I'll have to explain it to the Chief Medical Officer. What's her condition?"

"She's got a genetic disorder that manifests as a hyper-metabolic condition. She needs to consume at least fifteen thousand kCal a day to maintain minimum metabolic function. Sedating her has helped, but unless we can get her into suspension, she doesn't have much time left. She's severely malnourished."

"Holy frak," she whispered. "You've kept her alive for five weeks?"

"Is that how long it's been?" the man asked, shock nearly choking his voice out entirely.

"Five weeks and two days according to what we know," Ethan said. He pushed back in his seat and stood up. "We just tied off and are ready to come aboard."

Kicking the hatch release with his toe, he stayed back while it swung inward. Gasping, he blinked several times, trying to keep his firstmeal from reversing its progress through his digestive tract. "Whoa," he coughed.

"Sorry, it's the monkey," one of the men inside said as he reached up to help them climb down.

"Did it die?" Chelcee asked, pulling her medical respirator over her face, and pushing past him.

"We wish," the doctor said. He'd slipped through the door and was watching her swing down from the hatch.

Ethan thought about closing it behind her and getting his EVA suit on, but that would probably be rude. Instead, he bolted a grimace to his face and followed her into the lifeboat. His eyes felt like they were melting by the time he got his boots on the deck.

"I guess we got used to it," the man said, shrugging. "It really is a monkey."

"The *Aggie*'s captain said he had one as a pet," Ethan said. "I thought he was joking."

"Yah, and we ended up with it as a stowaway," the doctor said. He'd stepped out of the way but was watching Chelcee run a hand scanner over Tia. He stuck his hand out in Ethan's direction. "Adam Michaels."

"Ethan Walker," he said, his voice coming out like a pathetic squawk as he tried not to pull in any more air than necessary to make his vocal cords work.

"You said the captain made it?"

"He told us about the mutiny, and how the ExO blew up the ship," Chelcee said as she stepped back and studied the results of her scan.

"It wasn't a mutiny," the doctor said quietly. "It was pirates."

"He left that part out," Ethan said. "But his accounting has a bit of an odor to it. Especially after what the Chief Engineer had to say."

"That Valleri sold us out to the pirates?"

Ethan shrugged. "There will probably be a formal inquiry, but until we get the last of the boats accounted for, that's a hard day's haul from here."

Chelcee nodded. "I have to agree with Dr. Michaels. If we don't get her into cryo, she won't last more than another day. If that. We need to load them up and move. We can come back for the lifeboat, and the monkey, after we get her to the *Mendoza*."

"Understood," he said, tapping into his collarcomm. "Rescue Shuttle Six to *Mendoza*. We're about to be inbound with five survivors and one in critical medical condition. Request a team meet us in the hangar bay with a cryopod."

"Confirm that Rescue Six? Did you say a cryopod?"

"Confirmed," Chelcee said. "We're bringing a specialist doctor who can explain her condition."

"Copy Rescue Six, I'll run it up the stack and clear you for direct approach."

"Alright, let's get everyone up the ladder and out of the way so we can move her out," she said, waving her hand to shoo them away.

"I don't think we can get that diagnostic bed through the hatch," Ethan said, realizing it was too big to have come in that way either. He cocked his head to the side as he chewed that paradox over.

The doctor looked at him and smiled. "Don't hurt yourself. It was magic."

"The magic is that she's still breathing," Chelcee said. "We're going to have to carry her." She leaned over the bed, looking to make sure there were no tubes or straps holding her down. She was so frail she looked to be no more than skin stretched over a skeleton.

But her eyes flickered open.

"Hi there," the med-tech said gently. "I'm Chelcee. What's your name?"

"Tia," she whispered.

"We've been calling her Ammo," the doctor said, stepping up beside the bed and squeezing her hand gently.

"Ammo?" Ethan asked.

"It's a long story," he said. "But now that we're getting her out of here, all we have to do is figure out what gun to load her into."

Walker chuckled. "And which way to point it."

THE END

 Pick up **_Wings of Earth: 1 Echoes of Starlight_** the exciting first book in the Wings of Earth series.

https://mybook.to/woe1-paperback

PLEASE LEAVE A REVIEW

 Thank you for reading *Wings of Earth: Scatter the Winds*. If you enjoyed the story, please take a moment and consider leaving a review.

Reviews feed the creative souls of all authors and are invaluable in helping readers discover new books to experience.

Thank you. EMC

WHAT'S NEXT

One hundred thousand colonists can't disappear.

No bodies. No evidence of an attack. Just gone.

On what should have been a routine cargo run to the far edge of the Coalition, Captain Ethan Walker is carrying a payload of medical technology and two passengers returning home to Starlight Colony. When they arrive, they discover that everyone on the planet is missing.

The company he works for wants him to leave immediately, but he's obligated to report to FleetCom that the entire population has vanished. Captain MacKenna of the *Magellan* tells him to stay put until they can arrive to begin an official investigation.

Caught between his legal responsibilities and the need to know what happened, Walker has to resist increasing pressure to defy orders. Unfortunately, his passengers make a decision that forces him into doing the one thing he can't do.

Captain Walker must risk his ship and crew to return to the surface even though it may ultimately cost him everything.

http://mybook.to/woe1-paperback

OTHER WORKS

Atlas and the Winds
Book One: Stormhaven Rising
Book Two: Prometheus and the Dragon
Box Set: Atlas and the Winds

Shan Takhu Legacy
Book One: Legacy of Pandora
Book Two: Fulcrum of Odysseus
Book Three: Redemption of Sisyphus
Box Set: Shan Takhu Legacy

Wings of Earth
Book One: Echoes of Starlight
Book Two: Dust of the Deep
Book Three: Chains of Dawn
Book Four: Beyond the Edge
Book Five: Stranger Bedfellows
Book Six: Ghost in the Dark
Book Seven: Hope Dies Hard
Book Eight: Fastest Track
Box Set: Wings of Earth: Season One
Standalone: Scatter the Winds

Short Story
Ghostmaker

ABOUT THE AUTHOR

 Eric Michael Craig is a Hard Science Fiction writer living in the Manzano Mountains of New Mexico. He is the former Director of Research for a private consulting laboratory in Phoenix, where he experimented with inertial propulsion and power generation technologies.

Fascinated with the "cacophony of humanity," he dedicated much of his life to observing society and how people relate to each other and the world around them. Ultimately this drove him to write full time. When not writing, Eric is active in Intentional Community Design, plays guitar and bass, occasionally dabbles in art of various forms, and designs websites. He also owns way too many dogs.

Eric is a founding member of the SciFi Roundtable. The SFRT is an active online group dedicated to supporting indie and traditional authors by networking them with other writers and professional resources.

Connect with the Eric at: ericmichaelcraig.com
BookBub: https: bookbub.com/profile/eric-michael-craig

Sign up for Eric's newsletter to keep up on new releases and special features about his science fiction worlds and technologies.

Subscribe Link: https://www.subscribepage.com/s5g3p4

www.ingramcontent.com/pod-product-compliance
Lightning Source LLC
Chambersburg PA
CBHW050533260626
47157CB00004B/1580